215 Lexington A

By

Michael J P McManus

This book is dedicated to all creepy doll lovers everywhere

All characters featured in this book are fictional and any resemblance to persons living or dead is purely coincidental

215 Lexington Avenue

2017

Cover photo PublicDomainPictures.net

Cover design: Canva Designs

Also by Michael J P McManus

Paranatural Detective Agency Vol. 1 with David R Williams

Table of Contents

Chapter One

There it sat in an old rocking chair, unemotional, dusty, cobwebbed, unloved and forgotten. Forgotten over the years by its owner, never to be played with again, now that Wendy had new toys to play with, and the fact that she thought she was too big to play with dolls now.

The doll's bright blue eyes stared sightlessly into the dark murky corner of the attic where it sat forlornly. A large house spider crept silently along the cobweb it had spun on the doll's long black hair looking for trapped flies or other mites in its web.

Wendy now played games on either her X-Box or her tablet, while listening to music of her favourite band or singer on her iPod. Times change and a child's taste changes. Now and again her best friend Jodi would have a sleep over and the two of them would discuss which young singer they liked the best, or which game they would play and then spend hours shooting at zombies, they both loved The Walking Dead game and had become skilled in shooting down the zombie hordes.

Even though Wendy's parents thought the game might be too scary for a twelve year old girl, but the game never scared her and she would boast of how she would be able to save her mum and dad if there ever was a zombie apocalypse. Playing with silly dolls couldn't help save her mum and dad she thought as she zapped more of the walking dead! And anyway she never did like the doll that her Aunty Margaret had bought her, only playing with it for a few months then asking her dad to put it up in the attic where it has stayed to this day.

It was time for bed and Wendy had washed and brushed her teeth and said goodnight to her mum and dad and had gone up to her room. As much as she tried, Wendy couldn't sleep properly, she lay tossing and turning and was getting warmer under the heavy quilt. Lying on her back she opened her eyes, 'Hmmm it's no good I just can't sleep.' She thought to herself and lay still on her back in the hope that sleep would envelope her and carry her off into a land of happy dreams. It was while Wendy lay there she thought she could hear what sounded like scratching noises coming from the attic above her room, 'Oh no it sounds like we've got rats up there, I'll have to tell dad in the morning.' she thought to herself.

As she lay there she listened intently to the noise and realised that it sounded more like something being dragged across the ceiling, and then she thought she could hear footsteps, 'Hmmm it must be dad, he's always putting bits of junk in the attic.' And with that thought in her head Wendy drifted off to sleep.

The following morning Wendy rose out of her bed and scurried to the bathroom to shower and brush her teeth. Upon getting dressed she walked downstairs to be greeted by her mum Tina, her dad Bill, had gone off to work and as it was the school holidays, Wendy could spend time with her mum, which she loved doing. Being the only child Wendy's parents would spend as much time with her as possible and spoil her. 'Hi chicken how did you sleep?' asked her mum,

'Hmmm it took me a while to get to sleep with dad moving stuff around in the attic, but I fell asleep once he stopped.'

'What do you mean honey, your dad never went in the attic at all last night. Are you sure you weren't dreaming it.'

'No mum I was wide awake, it started off like scratching sounds and then dragging sounds as if something was being moved. Then I heard footsteps, and then it went quiet and I fell asleep.' replied Wendy.

Wendy's mum passed her a nice breakfast of bacon, sausage, egg and beans with toast and then sat down after getting her breakfast from the kitchen counter. 'Well I'll give the Pest Control Company a call to see if they can come and check the attic out and lay some traps, they sound like they are big rats.' her mum said with a smile, 'now eat your breakfast and once I've called pest control we can go to the beach once they've been and set the traps up.'

John Carter of the Pest Control Company walked into the kitchen, 'Well Mrs Rodgers, I've looked all around the attic and checked for any signs of vermin. Couldn't find anything, but I've set three humane traps which should do the trick. If there are any rats or mice in there, they'll be dealt with mark my words.' If you need any more help just give me a call, here's my card, saves you having to go through all the rigmarole of pressing one for this and two for that when you ring.'

Tina gave Carter seventy pounds and fifty pence via her bank card after he had worked out the total amount on his machine and printed off a receipt and wrote an invoice out for her as well.

'Well chicken, that's the noisy rat problem sorted, let's go the beach shall we and have us some fun in the sun!'

The beach of Coldport Town was one of the best in England and had been nominated best beach on no less than five occasions and won each time. Wendy and her mum crossed the road and after walking forty yards along the pavement they came to the concrete steps that would take them down to the golden sands where families were enjoying the school summer break playing with the children, making sandcastles and swimming. Couples were lying on towels sunbathing, the sky was a deep blue and the golden sun blazed down. The temperature was already in the high sixties and was going to get hotter by the afternoon.

Wendy and her mum held hands as they walked barefoot along the soft golden sand, both enjoyed the feel of the sand grains between their toes. 'Are you looking forward to going on holiday Wendy?' asked her mum.

'I am mum, I can't wait for dad to finish work, and I'm so happy that you're letting Jodi come with us.'

'Well we couldn't exactly keep you two apart could we and as long as her parents are happy to let her come on holiday with us, then we are honey. It'll be a great holiday as none of us have been to Cornwall before.' said Tina as she put her arm around her daughter and gave her a hug and a kiss on the head.

'Love you mum.' replied Wendy

'Love you back chicken.' replied Tina

As they continued down the stretch of beach they both talked about what they would do while on holiday and where they would visit. Ahead they saw an ice cream vendor and they both decided it would be a good idea to each have an ice cream.

'Two large cones, one chocolate and one vanilla please.' requested Wendy's mum and after receiving them and paying the two pounds and sixty pence for them they continued walking along the beach.

'It's days like these I love mum, no school, no homework, just loads of days enjoying myself with you and dad…and Jodi ha ha.' said Wendy licking the already melting ice cream. Later they went to Max's Fish Bar for dinner. Max served the best fish and chips around town and at three pound twenty a portion it was always busy.

Wendy's mum was a teacher at Coldport High School and at thirty eight years of age had been a teacher for ten of those years. She stood five feet seven inches in her stocking feet, a slim built woman with long blonde hair and deep blue eyes that peered out from a beautiful elfin shaped face. After a whirlwind romance and a proposal of marriage Tina became a mum at twenty six years of age. Wendy's dad stood six feet three inches with short dark hair and chiselled features and was an ex-rugby player and still worked out when he could. He worked as an analyst for a motor tyre making company called Deep Tread Super Tyres. His job was to analyse the components that were used to make the tyres and then get the prototypes tested to ensure they were good enough and safe enough to be put on the market. The company's fortunes had grown over the last two years leading to huge pay rises for bosses and workers. Bill Rodgers pay had increased tenfold and the house they had bought opposite the beach showed their wealth. With their combined wages they were able to buy the £500,000 house which was double fronted and boasted two large living rooms, a large country style kitchen, a large hallway with a solid oak staircase in the centre that lead up to the first floor that boasted a master bedroom with en-suite, and Wendy's bedroom also with en-suite and two guest rooms with en-suites. In the middle of the two guestrooms was an oak door which opened onto a small flight of stairs that lead up to the attic, which was big enough to walk upright and packed with all sorts of unwanted junk from their previous house. At the back of the house they had a conservatory and a large swimming pool, leading from the conservatory to the pool was decking that housed a barbeque and table and chairs.

Life was good for the Rodgers family and they had fitted in well with other wealthy home owners along that stretch of road and were often invited to house parties by some of the other home owners. Now to round off a year of hard work, the Rodgers were looking forward to a two week holiday.

Chapter Two

For the next two nights the scratching and walking around from the attic intensified disturbing Wendy's sleep. By Thursday morning she looked exhausted and ill, black circles were starting to form around her eyes through lack of sleep and her face was pale.

'Oh love you look dreadful are you coming down with a cold, go and lay on the sofa and I'll make you some breakfast.' said Wendy's mum as she went to get the quilt from her bed. By time she got back to her daughter was sound asleep. Wrapping the quilt around her she felt her forehead to see if she had a temperature. 'Hmm that's odd,' she's not over hot, thank goodness it's the school holidays and I can look after her.' thought Tina. Leaving Wendy to sleep, Tina went upstairs to change the bedding in her room and Wendy's room. As she was changing the bedding she thought she heard a noise, a loud creaking noise, no footsteps, yes that was it, footsteps coming from up in the attic. She stopped what she was doing and listened to the sounds emanating from the room above her head. 'My god, Wendy was right, it does sound like somebody is walking around up there.' she thought to herself, 'That's it; I'm going to take a look!' Briskly walking out of the bedroom, Tina walked towards the door that led up to the attic room. She stood outside and could still hear the noises from above. As quietly as possible she twisted the door handle and pulled the door open to reveal the wooden stairs leading upwards. Switching on the light switch she began to ascend the stairs, and as she got halfway up the noises abruptly stopped. Reaching the top of the stairs, she looked first to her left and then to her right, and then stepped into the large dusty room. She switched on the main light of the room and began to look around as she did she encountered the humane rat traps, all empty. 'Hmm that's odd.' she thought. 'What the devil could be making the loud walking noises up here?' Making her way to the corner of the room she spotted Wendy's old doll sitting upon an old rocking chair, dusty and cobwebbed, silently staring at her. 'Now I know why Wendy stopped playing with this doll, god she's creepy.'

Scanning the rest of the room she spotted an old radiogram that was an old piece of family furniture with a stack of old records on top of it, and a box of old photo albums, but she couldn't find anything that could have made the sound of footsteps and began to make her way back to the stairs leading down. As she started to walk away she heard a creaking noise behind her that made her freeze and stop dead in her tracks. Turning around to where she thought the noise was coming from, her eyes focused on the doll in the rocking chair and her blood ran cold, the chair was rocking and the doll was looking straight at her! Tina screamed and turning sharply ran as fast as she could down the stairs and through the open door. Turning she slammed it shut and turned the key in the lock. She then pulled the key out of the lock and pushed it into her jeans pocket.

As she entered the living room, she noticed Wendy was sitting up looking tired and puzzled. 'Mum I heard you scream, what's the matter?' asked Wendy. Her mum rushed towards the drinks cabinet and upon opening it she grabbed a bottle of whiskey, unscrewed the top and poured herself a generous shot of the brown liquid.

'Mum, mum, what's happened?' asked Wendy again.

'You were right Wendy, about the noises in the attic. I've just heard them and went to investigate what was making them.' She took another gulp of the liquid and the refilled the glass. 'I couldn't find anything at all, but when I was about to leave the attic I heard a creaking sound, it was the old rocking chair with your old doll sitting on it. It was rocking and the doll was looking at me, I couldn't get out of there fast enough!'

Tina asked her daughter if she felt well enough to go out and sit on the beach for a few hours, so she could calm down before Bill got home. Wendy said she could think of nothing better. As they sat on the beach they hugged each other and Wendy said that in a way she was glad that her mum had heard the noises, but not that she got frightened by it.

That evening when Bill got home Tina told Bill about what had occurred in the attic that morning. 'Oh come on now Tina, dolls just don't move on their own accord, or for that matter neither does a chair.'

'Well how do you explain the noises that sounded like footsteps I heard, and the fact that the noises have been keeping our daughter awake at night?' replied Tina now getting upset. 'Have you noticed how ill Wendy looks, she's not sleeping properly because she's hearing them too!'

'Okay, I'm sorry, come on let's both go up to the attic and take a look at this doll and chair. I'm sure there is a rational explanation for it all.'

As they made their way up the attic stairs and got to the top, Bill switched the light switch on, nothing, no light burned brightly as it did earlier when Tina went up there. 'Damn it was working earlier Bill, maybe the bulb has gone?' Bill felt around in a box to the left and found a Maglite torch, pushing the switch, the torch emitted a powerful beam of white light, 'Ah that's better, now let's take a look see.' said Bill as Tina grabbed his right hand for comfort. As they walked towards to where the doll and rocking chair was in the far corner, it began to move backwards and forward, Tina let out a scream, which made Bill jump. 'Hey honey, look here at the floorboard.' As he said that, Bill stood on a floorboard that was loose and the chair moved back and forward. 'Ah it's the floorboard that made the chair move, see?' Bill stood on it a few times and the chair rocked back and forth. 'Oh Bill I feel such a fool now, but, it still doesn't explain the sound of footsteps that Wendy and I have heard, does it.' replied Tina, 'and it's not rats otherwise they would be dead in the traps or they are incredibly talented and know how to avoid the traps.'

The couple returned back downstairs and decided to play a game with Wendy, the game it was a game where you have to answer questions and try and guess the link to the answers. It was one of Wendy's favourite games. As the night wore on all of them started to feel tired and decided to finish the game and head for their beds. 'Come on chicken, I'll tuck you in tonight.' said Wendy's dad, 'I haven't done that for a while have I?' Her parent's started calling her 'chicken' at a young age as Wendy loved the taste of chicken and would insist on having it nearly every week, even at Christmas time instead of turkey.

Wendy got herself ready for bed and when she was in bed she called her dad, 'All sorted now honey, teeth brushed and face washed?'

'Yes dad, all done.' replied Wendy now yawning not once but twice.

'I don't think it'll be long before you're asleep honey, and not long to go until our holidays and Jodi is staying tomorrow night too isn't she?' Bill tucked his daughter in and kissed her goodnight, 'Sweet dreams chicken and I'll be home early tomorrow I promise.'

Wendy smiled 'Night dad, I love you loads.' Within minutes Wendy was asleep and slept right through the night without any disturbances. Up in the attic the doll sat on the rocking chair staring blankly ahead as the large house spider furiously spun a fine silver thread around a fly that had landed in its web in the corner of the attic. This was the fifth fly to be caught in its web that day.

The following morning the Rodgers family all looked fresh and happy, even Wendy had managed to get up early so she could see her dad before he went to work, everyone was happy and excited that they would be travelling down to Cornwall very soon. That evening Wendy's friend Jodi was brought to the Rodger's house by her parents Mr and Mrs Johnson. Bill opened the front door for them all and welcomed them into the house. All shook hands and Bill invited them to sit down in the main living room. Tina and Wendy brought out the tea and sandwiches they had prepared for their guests. 'Now Tina you shouldn't have gone to the trouble.' said Norma

Johnson as she saw the two platefuls of sandwiches and a pot of tea being carried in on a silver tea tray.

'Nonsense Norma, you're old friends of ours and it's great that you're letting us take Jodi on holiday to keep Wendy company.' replied Tina as she poured tea from the pot into the cups then added milk and sugar to those that wanted it. 'It'll do the girl's good to be away for a couple of weeks in the sun, I've heard it's going to get hotter while we're away.'

Two hours later, Norma and Dave Johnson gave their daughter lots of hugs and kisses and said they would pick her up on Sunday morning as they were taking her to the zoo. 'Well girls, what games do you want to play tonight? As it's the weekend we can stay up a little later than usual.' asked Tina as she held up board games for them to pick.

Around eleven o'clock the girls were looking rather tired and decided to head for bed. 'I'm so looking forward to our holiday Wendy; we're going to have great fun together.' Jodi said as she got into her pyjamas and climb into the double bed she was going to share with her best friend.

'Yes it's going to be fantastic and dad said we are going to the Eden Project on one of the trips planned.' replied Wendy as she climbed into bed too. She wanted so much to tell her best friend about the strange noises but her mum asked her not to say anything in case Jodi got scared. She and Jodi said goodnight and Wendy switched the bedside table lamp off. Five minutes later both girls were sound asleep.

'Oh Bill I love you so much.' Tina said as her husband kissed and caressed her as they lay in their bed in the master bedroom. 'And I love you very much too honey, I love you more now than when I first met you.' Bill kissed her passionately and as he did so he cupped a hand around her breast and with his thumb worked her nipple until it became erect. Tina began to breathe heavily as she began to get more aroused, she could feel his hardness against her flat stomach 'Oh Bill, make love to me, now!' Bill entered Tina and she moaned loudly as he moved in and out rhythmically.

Later they lay in each other's arms and as their breathing slowed down they cuddled up together, 'hmmm as good as always love, you never fail to hit the right spot.' Tina kissed her husband and then leaned over to the bedside table to grab a glass of water. Taking a couple of mouthfuls she passed the glass to Bill, as he took the glass they both heard a noise above them. Slight scratching sounds at first which turned into heavier scratching sounds. 'What the hell is that?' asked Bill.

'Oh my god Bill that's the same sounds I heard the other day when I was making the beds. The same sounds that Wendy kept hearing.' Then they heard what appeared to be footsteps run across the ceiling above their heads.

'I hope the girls haven't gone up there and are messing about.' replied Bill as he got out of bed and proceeded to dress in a t-shirt and soft bed trousers which lay on a chair near the window. Walking to the bedroom door he quietly turned the door knob and opened the door. He waked down the landing expecting to see the door leading to the attic ajar, but it wasn't. He tried the door knob and the door was firmly locked. Puzzled he walked to his daughter's room and upon opening the door as quietly as he could he peeked inside, the girls were sound asleep. Closing the door he made his way back to the master bedroom, and Tina was sitting up in the bed 'Well honey, was it the girls?' Bill shook his head, 'No they are sound asleep and the attic door is locked, very odd indeed.'

As they snuggled up once again and were just about to drift off to sleep, an almighty thud hit the ceiling above them, 'Jesus! What in the hell was that?' shouted Bill. This time they both jumped up got dressed in their bed wear and headed for the landing, 'grab the attic key honey.' shouted Bill to Tina as he ran along the long landing. Wendy's bedroom door opened and both girls ran out, 'Dad, mum, what was that loud bang we heard?' cried Wendy as she ran into her father's arms. Tina arrived with the attic key to see her husband hugging both girls and as he did another loud bang emanated above them. 'Girls go back into your bedroom and stay there until me and your mum come and see you ok!' Both girls ran back to the bedroom door and Wendy turned and said, 'Dad be careful please.' Bill smiled and said he would. Wendy shut the bedroom door behind her and both she and Jodi dived under the quilt to hide themselves from whatever was making the loud bangs.

Bill ran back to the bedroom and returned moments later with a baseball bat, 'Right let's see who is in our attic shall we.' At six foot three inches and an ex rugby player, Bill Rodgers knew how to handle himself, but always had a baseball bat for protection...just in case. He eased the key into the lock and turned it twice, upon hearing the click of the lock he removed the key and pocketed it. Twisting the door knob he opened the door and flicked the light switch to illuminate the stairs leading up to the darkened attic. He remembered where he had left the Maglite after going up there last time, and as he got to the top step he stooped down to retrieve it. Switching the torch on, he panned the light's beam around the large room, 'Stay behind me honey, ok.' Bill began to walk across the floor looking to his left and then right, in front and behind him, but could see nothing tipped over, nothing had fallen onto the floor. More to the point, there was no sign of dust flying around the room, which it should have been if anything had been disturbed. As he scanned the room again, the light beam fell upon the face of the doll sitting in the corner, Bill jumped, 'Jesus! That scared the crap outta me!' he shouted. The doll sat there unblinking, unmoving, just staring at the couple now standing ten feet away from it. 'I told you it was scary Bill, that's why Wendy didn't want anything to do with it, she thought it was evil for some reason.' replied Tina

'Dolls can't be evil can they honey? I mean how can a doll become evil?' asked Bill as he slowly made his way towards the doll. Tina shuffled behind him and said that she had read a book called Demonic Dolls, which were true accounts of dolls that had become possessed by either a human spirit or a demonic entity. 'Surely you remember that film a few years ago called Annabelle and the one called Chucky?' replied Tina.

'But weren't they just made up stories babe, you know for the movies?'

'Well maybe Chucky was but Annabelle was based on a true story and the actual doll is in a paranormal museum somewhere in America, locked in a glass case.'

As they looked around some more they couldn't find anything untoward so they decided to go back to bed and make sure that the attic door was locked tight. Just as Bill was about to lock the attic door they both heard what sounded like a child laughing coming from the attic. Looking at each other both their faces drained of colour. 'Bill, there is no one up there except the doll.' whispered Tina, 'who the hell is laughing?' Bill took his wife's hand and headed for his daughter's room. 'Wendy, Jodi.' he whispered 'are you both alright?' Wendy popped her head out from under the quilt followed by Jodi,

'Yes dad we are, did you find out what made the banging noises and what…'

Wendy was stopped from finishing her question by two more loud bangs. 'Right kids, come on, we're going down stairs. Flicking on all the lights in the house to make them feel safer, Bill picked up the house phone and dialled 999, 'Police please, we think we have an intruder in the house up in the attic, can you send someone round please? Yes it's Bill Rodgers; address is 215 Lexington Avenue, Coldport, thanks'

Five minutes later two police cars pulled up and two officers knocked the door as the other two officers searched the grounds of the large house. Bill opened the door, Hello officers, thank you for coming so quickly, we have been hearing loud bangs in the attic room for the last half an hour but when my wife and I went to investigate it we couldn't find anyone there. Then as we went to make sure our daughter and her friend were alright, the loud bangs started again followed by loud laughter. So I decided to call you guys.'

The other two officers entered the house via the front door and reported to their sergeant that there were no signs of a forced entry on any of the doors or windows around the back of the house. As the sergeant was taking notes he asked the two officers to give PC Davies a hand searching all the rooms including the attic. PC Davies returned ten minutes later and asked for the key to the attic, Bill retrieve it from his pocket and passed it to the officer. Two minutes later he was back in the living room, 'Sir I think you had better come and see this, and you Mr Rodgers.' Bill looked at his wife, 'Stay with the girls' honey.'

PC Davies led them up the stairs and along the landing until they came to the attic door. The other two officers were standing in front of the now open door looking straight up. As the Bill and the two policemen joined them, one of them turned to Bill and asked, 'Is this some kind of joke sir?'

Bill looked up the attic stairs and as he did his blood ran cold, his face paled and he moved back slowly. At the top of the stairs stood the doll! Dressed in a black dress, its arms outstretched a smile on its face. 'No officer I can assure it is not a joke, that doll has been sitting on an old rocking chair in the corner of the attic for years. How it has got there is a mystery to me and my family.'

Sergeant Smith took control of the situation, 'Right you two up those stairs now and move that thing out of the way, we can't be getting scared of a child's toy now can we, come on, jump to it!' As the two officers made their way up the attic stairs the doll's head moved downwards and as it did its right hand moved and then downward its fingers outstretched and slashed at the first officer's face causing a deep scratch on his cheek. The officer let out a howl of pain and fell backwards into the officer behind him, causing him to lose his footing on the stairs and falling backwards.

'What in god's name has happened?' shouted Sergeant Smith when he saw the deep scratch on his officer's face.

'The, the, the doll...it attacked me!' cried the officer as he picked himself up. 'It looked at me and raised its arm and then, bam!'

Bill Rodgers shouted his wife to come up stairs, Tina raced up the stairs after telling the girls to stay where they were. 'What is it Bill, what's happened?'

'Tina can you help this officer, our demonic doll has just attacked him!' Tina took the officer into the bathroom and began to wash the blood off his face to she could have a better view of the scratch. 'Hmm it's quite deep and it looks like three scratches together. I can put some balm on it and then cover it. You may need to get it checked out though.'

The other officer tried to stand but his right foot had been badly twisted in the fall and he nearly fell over. Bill grabbed a chair from a bedroom and got the officer to sit on it. Sergeant Smith had just come off the phone, 'I've called for an ambulance, and they should be here shortly. But for now I am closing this door and locking it. Let's all get downstairs.' Both the sergeant and PC Davies helped the injured officer downstairs followed by Bill Rodgers, Tina and the officer who was scratched by the doll.

'Well Mr Rodgers I would say that you do have an intruder but not the normal kind. I would say you have an intruder of the paranormal kind sir.' said Sergeant Smith as he sipped at a mug of coffee while sitting in the kitchen with Bill and Tina. 'Is there anywhere your daughters can stay for the night?' he asked.

'Yes Sergeant, but only Wendy is our daughter; Jodi is her best friend and was staying over for the night.' replied Tina, 'but we can ask Jodi's parents if they could both stay at their house.'

'I think that would be for the best Mrs Rodgers. By the way do you both believe in the paranormal?' I only ask as I recall Mr Rodgers saying 'our demonic doll' earlier on upstairs.' asked the sergeant.

'Well Wendy is a believer, but I'm more of a sceptic, well at least I was until now.' replied Bill.

'Well in that case I will give you this card.' Smith opened his wallet and handed him a card on it was written Mr Joseph Daniels, Paranormal expert and Demonologist, and his phone number. Bill took it and read it then passed it to his wife. 'Are you a believer in the spirit world Sergeant Smith?'

'I am indeed and have been since I was a teenager. I've seen too many strange occurrences in my life not to believe. And trust me Mr Rodgers, it does exist and it can also be very, very dangerous. One day I may tell you about some of my experiences as I am planning to retire soon and when I do, I am going to become a full time paranormal investigator. I also know Joseph Daniels very well and know that he is holding a talk at the Neptune Theatre tomorrow night. I suggest you both go along and see him. He normally takes questions and offers his help as well.' concluded Smith

They both agreed they would and then Tina phoned Jodi's parents to see if they would be happy to have both Wendy and Jodi for the weekend. She said they would explain all when they got to their house with the girls. Meanwhile Sergeant Smith said he would stay at the Rodgers home with PC Davies until they got back to see if anything else occurred.

'So what do you reckon Tom, do you think the doll is alive or it's something else?'

Sergeant Smith looked at the young constable unsmiling, 'I'll tell you this Alan I've seen many a strange thing happen in my life time and you know that I believe in the paranormal don't you?' PC Davies nodded in the affirmative, 'Well all I'll say is this, somehow that doll in the attic has been taken over by an entity of some kind. Call it demonic, call it what you will, but it is possessed by something, and that something is evil beyond belief.'

Bill and Tina Rodgers arrived back home an hour later and found the two policemen had made themselves comfortable in the living room, with tea and toast. Sergeant Smith jumped up as the front door opened, 'Hi folks, hope you don't mind but we sort of helped ourselves to tea and toast. All has been quiet since you left. Are the girls okay at your friend's house?'

'Not a problem sergeant, we're just thankful that nothing else has occurred while we've been away. Yes Wendy and Jodi are fine, I think they were just happy to get out of the house for the night; they were really frightened by what happened. Wendy can't believe that her old doll could be the cause of everything that's occurred.' replied Tina as she took her denim jacket off and hung it on the coat stand.

'Would you two officers care for a drink, I know I could do with one after what we all witnessed before?' asked Bill as he moved towards the drinks cabinet in the living room. Before they could say anything Bill had poured four large glasses of whisky and handed them around. Sergeant Smith looked at PC Davies and nodded approval, 'Just don't tell the lads back at the station constable, cheers and thanks for allowing us to make ourselves tea and toast, it's been a long day.' said Smith raising his glass. 'So are you going to stay here tonight or somewhere else? I would strongly recommend that you do stay somewhere else tonight and then go and see Joseph Daniels tomorrow evening and ask for his help.'

'Well we can either stay at my mum's house tonight or a *Travel Safe Inn*, what do you want to do Bill?' asked Tina

'I would rather stay at a *Travel Safe Inn* tonight love, as I wouldn't want to worry your mum, not with her heart condition. If we can get it all sorted over the weekend then we needn't say anything to her.'

'That's a very good idea Mr Rodgers.' replied Sergeant Smith, 'Well I think if your about ready, it would be a good idea if we all leave together and lock the house securely.'

All agreed on this and Bill began to turn all the lights off around the house, as they were just about to leave they all heard loud banging coming from upstairs, 'My god, I'm glad we're leaving for the night, who knows what the doll can do.' said Bill as he opened the front door, 'Let's hope it doesn't get worse and annoys the neighbours.'

Smith turned the ignition on and steered the police car away from the house, he had offered to take the Rodgers to the nearest *Travel Safe Inn* for the night and said he would give Bill a call on his mobile, which Bill had given him while in the car. 'Keep safe and try and get a good night's sleep you two. You may be in for a long and frightening weekend, providing Joseph Daniels agrees to help you which he should. I'll tell you what folks, I'll go and see him myself tomorrow morning and let him know that you are going to attend his talk and I'll let him know what we have witnessed as well. Also, if he does agree to hold an investigation I wouldn't mind being in on it if that's okay with the two of you?'

Bill and Tina both agreed to what Sergeant Smith suggested and he dropped them off at the *Travel Safe Inn* on Kensington Road, 'Night folks and sleep well, I'll see you tomorrow at some point.'

Chapter Three

The following morning after a good night's sleep Tina phoned Wendy on her mobile to see how her night was. Wendy had explained that she had terrible nightmares about the doll chasing her through the streets shouting her name and brandishing a sharp knife. She also told her mum that Jodi had also had similar nightmares.

'That's it Bill we are definitely going to the paranormal talk tonight, both Wendy and Jodi have had nightmares about the doll. They are both scared and Wendy wants to stay at Jodi's parent's house until we get this doll thing sorted.'

'I agree Tina, whatever we need to do, we need to do it quickly.' replied Bill, and as they were about to go down for breakfast Bill's phone rang, 'Hello Bill Rodgers speaking.'

'Mr Rodgers it's Sergeant Smith here, did you both sleep okay? I've been in touch with Joseph Daniels and he's more than happy to have a chat with you during the interval of his talk.'

Bill explained to the sergeant that both his daughter and her friend had terrible nightmares about the doll chasing them with a sharp knife. 'It sounds like whatever it is, a demon, a negative entity, call it what you will, is trying to get to them both through their dreams. We need to act fast to stop the entity getting stronger.' replied the sergeant, 'I'll meet you at the theatre tonight, are you going back to the house at all today?'

Bill said that they were as they needed to get a change of clothes for themselves and for Wendy, then they were going to go back to the hotel as they had booked the room for the weekend anyway.

Joseph Daniels was a tall imposing man of thirty five, his dark hair turning grey at the sides; he was well built and wore black rimmed glasses which accentuated his dark brown eyes. His manner was mild and he had a quick dry sense of humour, good for investigations he would always say. He had been an investigator of the paranormal from the age of twenty and studied demonology at Coldport University from which he gained an honours degree. He had conducted over two hundred investigations with his team, the *Paranormal Findings Group* and had moved spirit on to the other side as well as debunking a number of so called hauntings in the area.

The first half of his talk dealt with five of his most successful investigations, introducing the members of his team who sat on a sofa on the stage. He played various EVP recordings that the team had captured via digital recorders and photos of what they believed to be spirits and spirit orbs. Mentioning an interval was due shortly he showed footage before the break of the cleansing of a possessed doll that had been attacking the daughter of the family. Various members of the public were shocked at the footage which showed the doll physically moving on its own accord and then a black misty shape shooting out of it and disappearing. The doll was once again a normal doll.

'Mr and Mrs Rodgers how are you both holding up' it was Sergeant Smith now looking totally different dressed in black jeans and a white shirt, a soft black leather jacket completed his attire.

'Sergeant Smith we didn't recognise you out of uniform, we're fine, and how are things with you?' asked Bill shaking the sergeant's hand, I'm grand indeed and off duty now until Monday, and by the way please call me Tom.' he said smiling at them both 'In that case Tom, it's Bill and Tina, said Tina smiling back. There was something about Tom Smith that Tina liked, a sense of trust and a feeling that he was going to do all he could to help them.

'Ah Tom, how are you my good friend?' came a voice behind the couple, it was Joseph Daniels and as he approached he held out his hand to shake Smith's hand. 'Great to see you made it to the talk, and at a guess I would say that this is Mr and Mrs Rodgers?' Shaking hands with the couple, Daniels explained to them that Tom Smith had given him a quick overview of what occurred at their house the previous evening. 'I have informed the team, and the good news is that we are all available to hold an investigation this weekend for you. I believe you want to join in with the investigation Tom?'

'If it's not a problem Joe, with what I witnessed last night I would like to.' Tom Smith replied before taking a drink from his bottle of Becks.

Sergeant Smith had given Daniels the Rodgers home address earlier that day and Daniels told the Rodgers that he and the team would call to their home around eight o'clock, that would give him time to prepare and get the team and equipment ready for the night ahead.

The talk on the paranormal by Joseph Daniels was a total success with over twenty questions being asked at the end and forty five of his books being sold as well as a number of framed spirit photos. Now Daniels and his team were preparing themselves for the investigation oblivious to the fact that they could all be in mortal danger once in the Rodgers home.

Bill and Tina arrived back at the hotel and headed for the dining area and ordered their meals and a bottle of white wine. As they sat at the table both were quiet for a few minutes. Tina looked at Bill while taking hold of his hand, 'Bill, do you think they will be able to solve the problem tonight as I'm worried what might happen to Wendy or Jodi after what Sergeant Smith told about how a spirit can haunt people in their dreams?'

Bill smiled at the woman he loved and caressing her hand he said, 'Honey there's one thing you can be sure of, I will not let anything hurt our daughter or you. And I'm certain that Sergeant Smith will do his upmost to help us as will the paranormal team. That Joe Daniels is very knowledgeable isn't he; he seems to know how to deal with a situation like ours. Well at least it looked like he can after watching that video footage earlier.'

The waiter brought their meals of roast chicken, potatoes, vegetables and gravy over to their tables and wished them both 'bon apatite' and left them to enjoy their meals. 'Tom said he will call here around seven forty five for our house keys and will keep in contact with us to let us know what is going on during the investigation.' said Bill after taking a sip of wine. 'He said it's for our own safety that we stay in the hotel tonight and keep in touch with Wendy as well.'

Finishing their meals they headed for the bar area where other guests were relaxing after their meals, either chatting or watching what was on the large flat screen TV at the time. The couple found a table for two next to one of the five large windows that looked out onto a pleasant vista of greenery and an ornate pond which had a large stone fountain at its centre. 'Well I'll feel better once we get the call from Sergeant Smith to say it's all over and we can go and collect Wendy and return to normal.' said Tina relaxing in one of the comfy chairs.

'Yes and then we will be able to concentrate of our holiday.' replied Bill while playing with Tina's long blonde hair. 'Let's have another bottle of wine and take it to our room, and cuddle up on the bed.' Bill got up and ordered another bottle of white wine and once he paid for it the couple headed off to their room for the night.

.....

Wendy was lying on her bed listening to the latest song by her favourite singer, with her eyes closed; she was totally relaxed and began to hum along to the song. As she lay there she felt safe and warm, then she felt her bed move and a coldness envelope her. Opening her eyes she looked around, nothing was there. So she closed her eyes once again and was about to begin humming along to the song again when she felt the bed move again, this time it felt stronger. Her eye lids sprung open and to her horror she saw her old doll standing at the end of her bed glaring at her, and brandishing a large kitchen knife in its right hand. 'Why did you leave me Wendy, I was given to you by Aunt Margaret, and you left me in that horrible attic, all alone! I hate you Wendy and now you must suffer for what you did to me!'

Wendy jumped up and as she did she awoke and terrified switched the night light on. There was no sign of the doll in her room and her tablet and headphones were on the other side of the room. 'I wish mum and dad were here with me.' she said out loud as tears began to trickle from her eyes. Wendy got up and walked over to the bedroom door, she was going to ask

Jodi's parents to take her to her mum and dad at the hotel. As he opened the door she screamed loudly, standing outside her door was the doll with the knife it its hand. Wendy jumped and again woke up, this time she raced straight to the bedroom door pulled it open and ran down the stairs to ask Jodi's parents to take her to the hotel where her mum and dad were staying.

Chapter Four

Sergeant Tom Smith pushed the brass coloured key into the lock of the front door of 215 Lexington Avenue, turned it twice and upon opening the door he entered the premises. It was now seven fifty five and he knew that Joseph Daniels and his team would turn up very soon, he switched on the hall lights and walking around the ground floor he turned on all the lights, to make it feel more welcoming. Walking back to the hallway he glanced up the grand staircase and a shiver ran straight down his back, he could feel the negativity emanating from the first floor, leading to the attic room. He walked into the kitchen and picked up a glass tumbler, walked to the sink and filled the tumbler with cold water. He gulped it down and then proceeded to fill the kettle full of water, a lot of coffee and tea was going to be needed tonight to keep them all going. Again he filled the tumbler full of cold water and as he was about to raise the glass to his lips he heard an almighty bang from above which made him jump and drop the glass into the sink causing it to smash.

Smith ran out into the hallway and another bang came, then from behind him came knocking on the front door. Turning he ran to the door and upon opening it was greeted by Joseph Daniels and his team, 'How goes it Tom?' asked Daniels as he entered the house. 'It's started already Joe; I've just heard two very loud bangs coming from upstairs!' replied Tom

Joseph ushered the team into the living room on the right, 'We'll use this room as our base camp.' Looking around he spotted a passageway to the kitchen, 'Ah that's good not far to go to make hot drinks either.' Tom had made drinks for them all and informed the team that he had witnessed many a strange thing over the years and was planning to become an investigator when he retired from the police force. 'Oh and by the way, tonight I'm an ordinary citizen so please call me Tom and not Sergeant Smith.' he concluded with a smile.

·····

Bill and Tina Rodgers had just finished making love and were cuddled up together when Tina's mobile phone began ringing, 'Hmm it can't be Tom reporting so soon can it?' asked Bill. Tina looked at the name which had come up on the phone's screen, 'it's Norma.' Clicking the answer button Tina held the phone to her right ear, 'Hello Norma, what's the matter? On no not again, yes of course bring Wendy to us. It's the *Travel Safe Inn* on Kensington Road. I'll wait at reception for you. See you shortly.' Tina hung up and told Bill what had happened. 'It's best to have Wendy here love, and then we know she's safe and she'll feel better sharing with us tonight.' replied Bill.

Norma Johnson dropped Wendy off at the hotel and after a quick chat made her way back home. Back in the hotel room Tina made Wendy a hot drink from the free drinks tray and both her and Bill tried to calm her, 'It's okay now love you're here with us and nothing is going to hurt you, we promise you chicken.' Wendy had not even changed out of her pyjamas as she was that scared of going back into the bedroom at the Johnson's home. She climbed into the bed with her mum and her dad slept in the single bed. 'Strange how we got a family room isn't it Tina.' said Bill, then yawning he closed his eyes and fell asleep. Minutes later both Tina and Wendy were fast asleep.

'Right everyone, if we're all ready, let's do this!' Joseph Daniels had organised his team into three small teams, Jack Temple and Jane Fitzgerald were to set up their equipment in Wendy's room and record anything out of the ordinary. Colin Davenport and Peter Cranford would set up in Bill and Tina's bedroom and Joseph, Tom and Alexis Bishop would concentrate on the stairs and landing and the attic doorway. None were quite ready to enter the attic just yet.

'The time is nine fifteen and nothing occurring yet.' commented Jack Temple into his voice recorder, 'I am now placing the recorder on top of the chest of drawers. If there is anyone here with us tonight please leave your voice into this machine with the red light on it. It will be able to pick up your voice.' Jane Fitzgerald walked around the room with a K2 meter in her hand hoping to pick up on electromagnetic energies in the room, nothing was happening.

Meanwhile in the master bedroom both Colin Davenport and Peter Cranford were conducting similar experiments. Tom Smith was sitting on a chair opposite the attic door, while Joseph Daniels sat on the right side of the landing, and Alexis Bishop sat on the left of the landing. All was quite in the house for the next forty minutes; Daniels looked at his wrist watch and said, 'Okay everyone let's end this session and have a break. Leave all recorders and camcorders running, but make sure you speak into the recorders to say what time it is etc.'

As the team gathered in the living room Alexis and Jane headed to the kitchen to make everyone a hot drink as they had all concluded that the temperature had dropped and all were feeling a little cold. 'So Alexis, what do you think of the house?' asked Jane as she washed the cups in the sink. Tom had already cleared all the broken glass out earlier and ensured none was left in it. Alexis Bishop lifted the now boiled kettle off its base and filled the teapot with the boiling water. 'It's an interesting one to be sure Jane.' she replied whilst stirring the teabags around in the pot. 'Tom's a nice man isn't he, and no sign of a wedding ring on his finger either.' Alexis continued with a smile on her face.

'Now then you naughty girl we're here to investigate ghosts and not men ha ha. But I know what you mean; he is quite a handsome guy ain't he. But don't tell Jack I said that will you ha ha.' replied Jane as she brought the clean cups over to her old friend. 'Wait till we sort this problem out then ask if he's seeing anyone at the moment, you never know do you.'

'As a matter of interest Joe, that footage you showed at the talk earlier today regarding the possessed doll, was the daughter seriously hurt by the doll?' asked Tom Smith as they all sat drinking tea and coffee and munching on chocolate biscuits.

'Put it this way Tom, it was one of the hardest and scariest investigations we've ever had to perform. Yes the girl ended up hospitalised for a few months and ended up in care of the state as her mind had gone. She is still in an institution and I believe it may take years for her to be allowed back home. Her parents were devastated and moved out of the area to be nearer the institution.'

'Jesus, let's hope we can sort the problem out here for the Rodgers, I believe their daughter has been having terrifying nightmares of the doll attacking her, and her friend has too.' commented Tom

'We'll do all we...BANG, BANG, BANG...BANG, BANG, BANG!

'My god let's get up there now!' shouted Joseph as he jumped up out of his chair.

Everyone raced up the stairs and found the attic door wide open and in front of them was a black mist that appeared to be forming into a human type shape. 'Jesus look at that!' shouted Tom

Joseph fished into his pocket and pulled out a crucifix and started reciting a verse he had learnt over the years.

'I cast you out of this home!
I cast you back into the place from whence you came!
I call upon almighty God to help us move you on!
I call upon Angel Michael and all the angels to cast you out!
The power of Christ compels you!

You must leave this house now!'

As Joseph spoke these words Jack Temple and Colin Davenport moved forward with vials of holy water and started splashing it at the dark shape, this enraged the entity and a force of energy managed to knock Colin Davenport off balance, it struck out at him again and he flew across the landing and down the flight of stairs landing in a heap at the bottom. 'Colin, are you alright?' shouted Jack Taylor There was no reply and Alexis ran down the stairs to help her companion. 'He's breathing but knocked out.' Alexis shouted back up to them.

Joseph repeated the verse and now Tom joined in repeating the lines after Joseph. The shadow person started backing off, backing off into the attic doorway; Tom kicked the door shut and twisted the key in the lock, but to no avail, the lock had been smashed open. 'What now Joe, how do we deal with something this powerful?'

'With our faith Tom and the help of the good Lord and Angel Michael, yes you're right it is powerful and we all need to be strong and not let it attack any of us again. Now let's check on Colin and help him into the living room.'

Tom, Joe, and Jack lifted Colin up and carried him into the living room and lay him on a large sofa. Jane had got a tea towel and dampened it, then placed it on Colin's forehead. A few minutes later Colin came round and complained that his right leg was hurting him. Tom felt Colin's leg and said it felt okay but that he might have fractured it. 'I need to cut your trouser leg Colin and take a look, are you happy with me doing this?' Colin nodded and after finding some sharp scissors in a kitchen drawer Tom cut the trouser leg upwards revealing

Colin's badly bruised leg, there didn't appear to be any sign of a broken bone but to be on the safe side Tom phoned for an emergency ambulance so the paramedics could check Colin out.

Ten minutes later the paramedics arrived and recognised Tom straight away. 'Sergeant Smith is everything okay, where's the patient?' asked one of the paramedics as he entered the house. Tom showed the paramedics to where Colin was laying on the sofa and asked if he needed to be taken to hospital. 'You say he fell down the stairs Sergeant Smith?' Tom nodded 'Well looking at Mr Davenport I would say that yes, he needs to be taken to hospital. Can any of you here come with us to keep him company?' asked the paramedic.

Alexis volunteered to go along to the hospital with Colin and said she would return once she heard if his injuries were serious or not.

The team reconvened in the living room to discuss what to do next, this time drinking glasses of brandy instead of tea as they were all shook up with the latest events at 215 Lexington Avenue. As the team sat quiet and deep in thought up in the attic the doll was back sitting on the rocking chair. On top of an old dresser sat an old music box, the type with a jack-in-the-box hidden inside it. This too was placed into the attic by Wendy as the face of 'Jack' scared her as much as the doll did. Music began to drift around the attic and the rocking chair began to move forward and backward as if the doll was listening to it and calming itself.

'Hey can you hear something?' asked Jane, 'it sounds like music and something else…creaking, yes creaking noises.'

'Hopefully our recorders are picking all this up and the camcorders on the landing picked the shadow person up.'

replied Joseph Daniels, 'Let's sit awhile and gather our strength. I've a feeling we've got a long night and a hard battle ahead of us.'

Back at the *Travel Safe Inn* hotel the Rodgers family slept soundly unaware of the horrors unfolding in their house at that moment. Wendy was snuggled up to her mum but still had a frown on her forehead as if she was still having bad dreams. Bill Rodgers tossed and turned and finally after a few hours' sleep lay on his back with his eyes closed but his mind racing. He would get in touch with his sister tomorrow to ask her where she got the doll from in the first place.

In the attic the doll stopped rocking as the music box stopped playing, its porcelain hands resting on the chairs armrests, its body encased in the long black Victorian dress. Slowly but surely the doll lifted itself up and off the chair, as it moved forward the chair rocked once, twice, three times, and then stopped. The doll began to walk slowly across the attic floor, its porcelain face grimy with dirt, but its blue eyes intense. An evil smile split its once pretty face and now pure hatred came into its whole being. The negative entity was no longer a shadow person but a force of pure hatred which had the power to control and move inanimate objects. As it reached the top of the steps of the attic its once pretty face looked down towards the doorway, the door opened quietly. It began to walk down the attic steps and stood in the doorway as if listening. Turning right it walked across the landing towards the top of the grand staircase. The doll began to descend the stairs, and at the bottom it stopped. Its head turned slowly left and then right and then moved slowly towards a doorway which lead into the kitchen.

'Well, how are we all feeling now, should we try again to move the entity over to the light?' asked Tom.

'But what if it doesn't want to be moved over to the light, after all it is a negative entity?' replied Jane, now looking somewhat fearful of what may happen next.

'We have got to try and be positive Jane for the sake of the Rodgers family and for our own safety. Listen I know you're scared, I think to some degree we all are after what happened to Colin. But we must do this and we need to start again right now.'

Jane nodded and said that she just needed to get a bottle of cold water from out of the fridge in the kitchen. 'Won't be a minute, don't leave this room without me please.' All nodded and Jane walked through the archway and down the short passageway to the kitchen. Going to the fridge she opened it and bent slightly to grab a bottle of cold water from the send shelf down. Closing the door she turned and screamed as she saw the doll in front of her, it looked at the table and then at a sharp bladed knife. The knife flew from the table and just missed her and embedded itself in the wall next to a large Welsh dresser; Jane screamed again and ran towards the living room via the passageway. Halfway down the passageway the others were running towards her, 'Go back, for pities sake go back! Into the other living room now!' she yelled as she ran passed them, and as she ran she felt dampness in her jeans. Stopping inside the other room, she looked down to see that she had peed herself through fear. The others gathered in the living room, 'Jane, Jane what happened, what was it you saw? My god Jane you've peed yourself honey?' asked Jack as he rushed over to his girlfriend.

'It was the doll, it was in the kitchen and somehow it managed to throw a knife at me, luckily it missed me. But the look on its face, my god, I'll never forget it. I'm sorry guys but that's it for me. I'm leaving; I never expected it to be this bad. Whatever is in this house is demented and totally evil, and if it can control not only a doll but make things move by what appears to be thought alone, well that's it for me. Sorry but I've never been so scared in my life hence me peeing myself.' Jane then burst into tears and started shaking with fear.

'Jack can you take Jane home please and stay with her until she calms down.' asked Joseph. 'We will be three people down if Alexis doesn't come back tonight, Jane will you be okay if Jack comes back?'

Jane nodded 'I'll get Jack to drive to my sister's house she should let me stay there the night with her.'

'Right let's go to the kitchen and see if the doll is still there.' said Joseph as he closed the front door behind his two friends after watching them get into Jack's car and drive away. Joseph, Peter and Tom made their way to the kitchen to find it was in darkness. Flicking the light switch on the wall made no impression at all, the room remained in darkness. Tom pulled his Maglite torch out of the back pocket of his jeans and turned it on, its powerful beam lit up the room, to reveal nothing, and there was no sign of the doll anywhere in the kitchen. 'Do you think Jane may have been mistaken?' asked Peter. 'I don't think so, replied Tom; look over there on the wall near the dresser.' Embedded in the wall was a twelve inch bladed knife. Tom walked over it followed by the other two men. 'It's embedded in the wall by at least an inch and a half. Bloody hell that has been done with some force, no wonder Jane was so scared, the poor girl. She's lucky to be alive!'

'But where the hell is the doll if it's not in here?' replied a now scared Peter.

'It's either back up in the attic or it is hiding in another room down here.' replied Tom as he made his way through the kitchen door which lead back into the hallway. Suddenly all three men heard thunderous banging from upstairs.

'What the hell?' screamed Peter now backing up towards the front door. 'I'm not staying here to be attacked by that thing, sorry guys but I'm going too.' Peter ran to the front door turned the door knob but nothing happened, 'Shit, shit, it's locked, Tom where the hell is the key?' he screamed. Tom ran over with the key and turned it twice, nothing happened. 'No, no, don't say we can't get out, please don't say that!' cried Peter.

The banging filled the house and sent shivers down the three men's backs. 'Tom, I think this is your call.' said Joe.

Tom looked at Joe, 'What the hell do you mean Joe, it's my call?'

'Call your colleagues for back up; we're going to need them, right now!'

Tom pulled out his mobile phoned and taped a key which took him straight to police headquarters. 'Alan, it's Sergeant Smith here, myself and two others are at 215 Lexington Avenue, we need back up right now and bring the door breaker when you get here. And get the sirens and blue lights going we need you here now!'

A few minutes later the front of 215 Lexington Avenue was filled with flashing lights and policemen were racing towards the house, PC Davies looked at his fellow officer but before he told he fellow officer to use the door breaker he tried turning the doorknob, the front door opened straight away. Rushing into the house PC Davies found his colleague and two other men, 'Quick PC Davies let's get out of here.' shouted Tom

Smith. As they got down the pathway, they all stopped still as the front door slammed shut behind them. 'Are you alright sir?' asked PC Davies

'This is something I feel we are not going to be able to control or banish from this house. It is pure evil constable, pure evil, and I don't think we are strong enough to move it on.' replied Tom Smith 'Joe, do you and Peter want to come back to my house or are you going back to your own homes?'

'I think going back to your house is a good idea Tom, I can phone Jack and let him know what's happened. Peter can you phone Alexis and tell her if she's not staying at the hospital to go straight home?' asked Joseph as he stood looking at the house on Lexington Avenue.

'It might be a good idea if Jack and Alexis came back to my house too Joe, I've got enough room, my parent's left me their house in their will when they both passed away and it is quite a large house, so I've no problem about you all staying at mine for the night. We can all sit and discuss what the hell just happened and what we are going to do to help the Rodgers.' said Tom Smith as he got into his car. Joseph and Peter got into Joseph's car and as they all pulled away from the house none of them noticed the doll looking out of the attic window and standing next to it were two dark figures also watching them leave.

The doll stood in front of the attic window its deep blue eyes looking out, it then slumped to the ground as the third entity released its grip on it. The energy around the attic room began to build up and things began to move and vibrate. The old music box began playing a tune and the jack-in-the-box began popping up and down getting faster and faster as the entity energies grew stronger and stronger. Items of furniture began to levitate off the floor and two disused mirrors shattered, the fragments of glass shards flying through the air and puncturing walls, ceilings and old toys.

The energies grew ever stronger and every door in the house began slamming shut then opening and slamming shut. Lights went on in all the houses in the street as people were awakened by the loud banging, but most of all, by the inhuman screams coming from 215 Lexington Avenue.

Then as quickly as the energies built up, it petered out to a whisper and once again the doll was sitting in its rocking chair and the music box played its sweet tune. The spirits had made their presence known and waited patiently for the ones who wanted to move them into the light to return.

The following morning after only a couple of hours sleep Sergeant Smith headed into town to check on the Rodgers family and inform them of what happened the previous night. Entering the hotel he walked to reception and asked if the Rodgers family were down from their room yet. 'I believe they may be at breakfast sir.' came the response. Sergeant Smith was in his casual wear as he was still off duty and as he walked through the dining area he spotted Bill Rodgers and his family sitting at a table for four.

'Good morning folks how are we this morning and it's good to see Wendy is with you. Did you sleep well last night?' he asked

'We did Tom, but it looks like you've been up all night, you look shattered.' Tina replied as she was tucking into a full English breakfast.

'I managed to grab a couple of hours sleep, but I really needed to come and see you folks about last night.'

'Would you care for a cup of tea Tom?' asked Bill as he poured himself a cup

'That would be great thanks. Last night we had to call a halt to the investigation. One of Joseph's team was injured and ended up in hospital, and one of the girls narrowly missed having a knife stuck through her, and she refuses to go back to your house. I'm telling you this while Wendy is here with you as I recall what you told me about her nightmare. Whatever is in your house is controlling the doll and it can move objects as well. Another member of the team wanted to leave and upon trying to open the door he found it locked. Even using the key wouldn't open it. In the end I had to call the station for back up to get us out, and when they arrived they were able to open the door from the outside without any problems.'

'Oh my god, that is awful Tom, is the person who got injured going to be alright?' asked Tina

'Yes, Alexis, one of the team members went to the hospital with Colin, the guy that was injured and said he had suffered bad bruising to the legs, arms and ribs, and concussion. He should be out in a day or two. The rest of the team except Jane, the girl who won't go back into the house are all staying at my house. We are going to hold a meeting this afternoon to see what we can do. I'm going to book a week's leave as I don't think this will be solved any time soon.'

'But what about us Tom, when do you think it'll be safe for us to go back to the house. We can afford to stay here at the hotel for a week, but we are booked to go away on holiday in two weeks.' asked Tom as he finished off his breakfast.

'All I can say Bill is to stay here for now and as soon as we have dealt with the entity and banished it, I will let you know.

I'll keep you in the loop anyway regarding what is happening. I think Joseph mentioned getting a priest in to perform an exorcism of sorts, as it is beyond us at the moment. I'll know more after we have our meeting later. But for now I need to go and see my boss and explain to him why I need time off earlier than planned.'

Tom stood up and shook Bill and Tina's hand and gave Wendy a big hug, 'Now listen to me young lady, I'll get this problem sorted for you and your mum and dad and once it's all sorted you'll be able to go back home. Is that okay?'

Wendy hugged Tom back and smiled, but then looked serious, 'Tom, what if the entity doesn't want to leave, what then?'

'Myself and the team of investigators won't let them stay honey, and that's a promise.' Tom kissed Wendy on the cheek and ruffled her hair, and bid the family farewell.

Tom drove to police headquarters and met up with Superintendent James Fisher and explained everything to him regarding the events at 215 Lexington Avenue. Fisher had known Smith for a number of years and held him in high esteem and had no problem with him taking a week's leave. He even told him that if he needed a further week to let him know. Fisher had already been given a report on the disturbances by PC Davies, and even offered the help of back up if needed again.

Tom Smith drove home and checked the time on the car's clock, it read ten thirty five and he stifled a yawn, he knew he would need a power nap before he, Joseph and the others had their meeting. As he entered the house he could hear raised voices coming from his living room, removing his jacket and hanging it up he stood and listened to what was being said.

'I really don't want to go back there either.' said one voice

'But we need everyone in the team if we are to beat the entity!' another voice replied.

Tom recognised the two voices; one belonged to Peter, the other to Joseph. Upon entering the room the talking stopped and the team turned to look as Tom. 'Is there a problem Joseph?' asked Tom.

'You could say that Tom, Peter doesn't want to go back to the house again after what happened last night, and Jane is taking time out and is demanding Jack does as well, which leaves three of us, Alexis, myself and you Tom.'

Tom yawned loudly, 'Let me get an hour's sleep and I'll see what I can do Joe.'

Chapter Five

Tom slept for nearly two hours and by the time he'd showered and dressed it was approaching one o'clock. He walked into the living room and noted that only Joseph and Alexis were in the room. I take it that Peter and Jack have gone home then?' asked Tom.

'Yes Tom, but I think Jack really wants to help us defeat the entity as he knows what it is like to be tormented by a negative spirit. He is going to talk to Jane about it and let me know.' replied Joseph.

'And what about you Alexis, are you happy you stay on and help us?'

'Yes Tom I am, I have a young cousin that I adore, she's seven years old and I know for sure that I wouldn't want her to be tormented by something the way Wendy is. You can count on me Tom!'

Tom picked up his phone and said, 'I have a feeling that a young police constable I know would like to help us. You may remember him from last night Joe, PC Davies.' Tom tapped in his colleague's private number and held the phone to his ear, 'Alan its Tom Smith, how are you, good to hear mate. I have a question to ask you. How would you like to help us with the problem at 215 Lexington Avenue? A few of the team members have bailed out and we are short on numbers to do what we have to do. You would! Great but it would mean asking Superintendent Fisher for time off as it could take a few days. That's fantastic buddy, I really appreciate it, and fingers crossed all goes well with Fisher, bye for now.'

Tom was just about to go into the kitchen to make tea for everyone when he heard the front door knocker banging. Opening the front door he was greeted by Jack Temple and Jane Fitzgerald, 'Hey Jack, Jane, come in, come in, great to see you both.' Tom led them to the living room and both Joseph and Alexis couldn't believe that both Jack and Jane had come back to Tom's house.

'I thought you guys had had enough of ghost hunting to last you a lifetime?' said Alexis as she hugged them both.

'Well we both got talking and I knew Jack didn't want to let you guys down, and after all we are doing this to help people right!' replied Jane, 'so I agreed to carry on and help, as long as that creepy doll doesn't come anywhere near me.'

Five minutes later Tom returned from the kitchen carrying a tray with two pots of tea and five mugs and two plates of sandwiches. 'I'm so grateful that you have both returned to help, I really mean that. It means a lot to me as I like the Rodgers family and have vowed to help them. I'm hoping that a colleague, Constable Alan Davies will be able to help us as well. Alan was the guy that helped us out of the house last night along with the back-up team. He was also at the house with me on the Friday night after Bill Rodgers put the call in to the station.'

Half an hour later there came a knock at Tom's front door, upon answering it, Tom was pleased to see Constable Alan

Davies standing on the threshold out of uniform, 'Alan, great to see you, come in buddy.' Tom led his work partner into his living room and introduced him to Joseph Daniels and the remaining members of his team. Alan shook hands with them all and then told Tom that Superintendent Fisher had allowed him a week's leave to help the investigation.

'So when do you want to go back into the house and try and get rid of the entity and the doll?' asked Alan

'I think the sooner the better, replied Joseph, as long as everyone is okay with that, especially after last night's encounters.'

All agreed that the sooner they went back the better, so that once the house was clear of all negative energies, the family could move back in. 'I've promised the Rodgers daughter that I would personally get rid of the doll and the jack in the box that apparently is also in the attic. Wendy is scared stiff of both items.' said Tom as he collected all the cups and placed them onto the tray with the teapots and empty plates and took them into the kitchen.

......

Bill Rodgers got himself ready and asked both Tina and Wendy if they were sure they didn't want to come with him to see his sister Margaret, they both said no and as it was a nice sunny day Tina was going to take Wendy to the zoo for a few hours. Bill was determined to find out where his sister had bought both the doll and the jack in the box, and if need be go to wherever she bought them and ask about their origins. Bill wanted his family to be safe and life to get back to normal as soon as possible.

At forty three years of age Margaret Rodgers was known as the village spinster as she had never married, and seemed to prefer her own company. There was talk in the village that Margaret was a lesbian, but no one in the village of Boxley could prove or disprove it. She was a striking looking woman with dyed red hair which hung just below her shoulders, sharp defined features and grey eyes. She ran an aromatherapy shop in the village and did reasonably well for herself, and had a full time assistant working for her called Monica.

As Monica was setting up a new display of scented oils the chimes above the shop's front door chimed signalling that someone had entered. 'Good morning sir, how may I help you?' she asked the tall well-built man that had just walked in.

'Hi there I'm looking for Margaret, is she around?'

'Yes she is in the back store room, who may I say is asking for her?'

'Tell her it's her brother Bill please, it's quite urgent I see her.' replied Bill and stood waiting as the assistant went to fetch his sister from the store room.

'Bill what a pleasant surprise, where's Tina and Wendy, nothing wrong I hope?' said his sister as she walked into the shop and then gave him a hug and a kiss on the cheek.

'Is there somewhere we can talk, it's a private matter?'

'Yes we can go into the kitchenette just off the back store room. Monica can manage on her own for a while.'

Margaret showed Bill into the kitchenette and shut the door behind her, 'Take a seat Bill, would you like a cup of tea?' Bill nodded and Margaret put the kettle on and placed tea bags into two mugs. 'So what brings you all the way here Bill, nothing wrong at home I hope?'

Looking his sister in the eye Bill nodded and said 'Yes there is something wrong at home, and I think it has something to do with that doll you bought Wendy as a gift quite a few years ago.' Bill went on to explain all that had happened over the last week at the house and now wanted to know where she had purchased the doll and if she had purchased the Jack in the box from the same shop.

'Oh my god Bill, you don't think that the doll is possessed do you? Things like that just don't happen...do they?' I bought it from a shop called *Back in Time* it's an old antique type shop. I saw it and couldn't resist getting it for Wendy at the time.'

'Do you know the history of the doll, such as who the shop owner bought it off, how old it is that sort of thing?'

'I'm sorry Bill I don't, but I still might have the receipt somewhere, maybe if I find it we could go to the shop and see if the owner remembers me buying the doll and ask if he remembers where he got it from. It's a long shot I now but I'll do anything to help, you know I will.' replied a now distraught Margaret.

'Will it be open today, it is Sunday after all?'

'Yes he opens from twelve noon till four o'clock on a Sunday. Let me check to see if I can locate the receipt, I usually keep all my receipts in an old biscuit tin, ah here we are, let's have a look.'

After sifting through the tin of receipts Bill was about to give up when he picked up four receipts and the third one he looked at had the name *Back in Time* at the top of it and the item, 1 Doll and the cost, £25.00 typed onto it, 'Here it is, found it!' cried Bill, 'Come on let's go and find out what we can about that damned doll!'

Joseph Daniels informed the team that he had been in touch with Father Gabriel, of the Star of the Sea Catholic church in town. He mentioned that they had worked together a few years ago on an exorcism; the head of the church wasn't too impressed with Father Gabriel, but after making his case regarding the need for a priest who could perform an exorcism in that part of England, the church allowed him to continue but in his own right and without the help of the church. 'Father Gabriel said he would meet us here around seven o'clock tonight. He has to prepare himself by meditating for a few hours first. Do we have any background information of the house or the doll Tom?' asked Joseph.

'Bill Rodgers informed me this morning when I went to see the family that he was going to see his sister, who lives in the village of Boxley, apparently that is where his sister purchased the doll prior to giving it to Wendy as a birthday present. Hopefully he will find out about the doll and get in touch with me as soon as he can.' replied Tom

Back in the village of Boxley, Bill and his sister Margaret walked into the *Back in Time* shop and Margaret introduced herself and her brother to the shop owner. 'I'm hoping you can help me find out some background history of a doll I purchased here a couple of years ago. I have the receipt here and I can describe the doll to you.' said Margaret handing the receipt to the owner.

'I think I have a photo of it on my phone.' Bill said as he took his phone out of his pocket and began scrolling through his many photos. 'Yes here we are this is the doll that my sister bought from here.' Bill showed the owner the photo of the doll, 'Do you remember selling it sir?'

Studying the photo on Bill's phone the shop owner took a few moments, 'Ah yes the Katie Doll and it dates back to the Victorian era. Let me see if I can find the right book about Victorian dolls which should have some information about the Katie Doll. The shop owner went behind the counter and looked amongst the shelving on the back wall. 'Here we go, now let's see if it has a section about the Katie Doll in here. Looking through the contents the shop owner spotted the chapter he was looking for. 'It's five pages long but it goes into great detail about the doll.' he said passing the book to Margaret.

'Would you mind if we photographed each page, so we can transfer the pages to a laptop?' asked Bill.

'Not a problem at all sir.' replied the shop owner, 'The doll was brought in here quite a long time ago now and I think the person who brought it in said they lived in a Victorian house on Lexington Avenue. I can't recall the number of the house though.

Bill stopped taking photos of the book's pages, 'Did you say a large Victorian house on Lexington Avenue. I ask because I live in a large Victorian house on Lexington Avenue, and I've always wondered who lived there originally.' said Bill looking quite shocked.

'You will more than likely find that information in Coldport Library, I believe they have a very old book chronicling the town's history right back to medieval times, which I believe is when the town was but a small hamlet.'

As they left the shop with the shocking news about the house, Bill was determined to find out more about his house and who lived there. But how would he be able to go to the library, it was Sunday and it would be closed and he would have to go back to work tomorrow. 'I'm going to have to try and get to the library tomorrow, maybe finish work early or something.' said Bill to his sister as he drove her back to her shop.

'I could do it for you Bill, I could ask Monica to mind the shop and I could drive into Coldport and look for the information for you. I could spend most of the day in there. That's if you wouldn't mind Bill?'

'You would do that for me Margaret, I mean take time off from your work?'

'Of course Bill, after what you, Tina and Wendy have all been through, I feel somehow responsible with giving the doll to Wendy, I'm so sorry Bill.' Margaret began to sob and Bill pulled the car up outside her shop. 'Hey come on now sis, it's not your fault, you weren't to know about the doll.' Bill hugged his sister tightly and told her that he would let Tina and Wendy know that she will be in town on Monday, 'You never know they may give you a hand looking for the information.'

·····

Back at Tom Smith's house the team waited patiently as the time dragged on. Tom asked if anyone was hungry and when they all said yes, he ordered five large pizza's for them to share, along with bottles of cola. Once all the food was consumed, Joseph suggested that they all try and relax as best they could as they would need all their strength for the long night ahead. Tom's eyes felt heavy and he closed them and relaxed in his favourite armchair, but his mind wouldn't switch off, he couldn't stop thinking about the night before and how dangerous it was for all of them. Suddenly he heard a pounding in his head, where was it coming from he thought. Opening his eyes he saw Joseph rushing out the living room and then the sound of the front door opening, he then heard Joseph speaking to someone. Standing up he yawned loudly and rubbed his eyes, the saw Joseph walk into the living room accompanied by a tall dark haired man sporting a short dark beard, a dark mid length leather coat, dark trousers and a black shirt.

'Tom, everyone, may I introduce Father Gabriel, or Gabe as he likes to be called by friends.' Everyone shook hands with the priest and Tom asked if he would care for a drink of tea or coffee. 'Would you have something a bit stronger Tom, maybe a whiskey?' asked Gabe.

'Why sure, would anyone else like a drink?' all nodded except Joseph, 'Thanks but no thanks Tom, I gave up drinking five years ago, a cup of tea if you don't mind making me one?'

'I'll give you a hand Tom,' said Alexis as Tom moved towards the kitchen.

In the kitchen Tom made a cup of tea for Joseph. 'Do you think we'll be safe tonight Tom, I mean after last night's happenings. I'm a bit worried that someone else might get hurt.' asked Alexis.

'I don't know Alexis; I truly hope that we will all be safe tonight and that having Father Gabriel with us we will help matters.' Replied Tom, 'let's all have a drink and see what the plan is, and don't worry Alexis I'll make sure you don't come to any harm tonight, I promise.' Tom gave the pretty young lady a smile and then walked into the living room with her. Alexis' heart skipped a beat as she followed him into the room.

'When we get into the house, be on your guard at all times, the demon, which I think it certainly sounds like will be ready for us, and will be cunning as you've already found out. We will try and contain it in in the attic, and when the time is right we will perform the exorcism. You will all have to be strong and I will need you Joseph to work alongside me like last time. I cannot express to you all of the danger we face tonight. We are going to have to watch everything carefully, as the demon, as some of you have found out already, can move objects by thought and with great force. Do we know anything about the history of the house Tom, or the doll that is being controlled?' asked Father Gabriel after giving his advice to all.

'Bill Rodgers who is the current owner of the house has been to see his sister today. She was the lady who bought the doll for his daughter Wendy, not realising what was going to happen. I don't think he knows the history of the house though Father.'

'Please Tom call me Gabe, or I'll have to start calling you Sergeant Smith, and that would be too formal ha ha.'

'Tom laughed as did the rest of the team, 'Gabe it is, and thank you so much for helping us, I really mean that.' said Tom shaking Gabe's hand again.

'Do we need to take any equipment with us tonight Gabe, or should we just trust our instincts and you're good self?' asked Jane Fitzgerald, now feeling more relaxed that they had a man of God helping them.

'It depends really, if you want to record anything for prosperity and use your gadgets to detect where the entity is then it's really up to yourselves to decide, I've no problem at all with equipment being used.' replied Gabe, 'Before we go I will perform the prayer of protection for us all. I will ask you all to stand in a circle and join hands. I will then call upon Angel Michael to cover us in his white light of protection throughout the whole night and also to cover the house we are going to in his white light. We should prepare ourselves now, by that I mean get whatever equipment you want to take with you and then we all need to sit quiet and relax and all visualise the white light and its warmth around us.'

The clock on the wall in Tom's living room struck eight o'clock and Father Gabriel got the team to stand in a circle holding hands and began to recite the prayer of protection. Once it was over, they all hugged each other and vowed to watch each other's backs while at the house. Getting into two cars, the investigators and the priest made their way to 215 Lexington Avenue.

······

Back at the hotel Bill met Tina and Wendy in the dining area and ordered a meal as his wife and daughter had started eating their evening meal. He told them about what he had learnt about the doll and especially about the house. 'Yes Margaret is coming up tomorrow and going to spend the day in the library looking for everything she can about the house and its previous owners. I don't know yet if it is our house that the shop owner mentioned but it seems too coincidental not to be.'

'We can meet Margaret tomorrow if you want us to Bill, I know it's not her fault that the doll is possessed by something, and it would keep our minds occupied until we hear from Sergeant Smith. He phoned while you were at Boxley and said that they would be going back to our house tonight and that they have the help of an exorcist, a Father Gabriel.'

Bill was just about to reply when his mobile rang, 'Hello, Bill Rodgers, Tom it's good to hear from you. I believe you're going to the house tonight. Yes Tina told me you'd phoned earlier. Yes I've managed to get some info about the doll and it seems the house and doll could be connected from a long time ago.' Bill listened to Tom speaking and replied, 'Yes I'm going to transfer the info about the doll onto my laptop and see if I can find anything of interest. Apparently it was a Katie Doll, whatever that was. Yes I'll let you know if I find anything relevant. You too, and take care, all of you, bye.' Tom replaced the phone in his pocket and he and his family went back to their room.

.....

'Right let's see what is so special about Katie the doll shall we?' said Bill as he finished downloading the information from his phone to his laptop. While Bill read the pages about the doll, Tina and Wendy played cards to pass the time away. Bill had a large glass of red wine as did Tina, while Wendy drank a soda. 'Anything yet honey?' asked Bill's wife as she came back from using the bathroom. 'No nothing yet, Katie the doll just seems to be just that, a doll, which at the time was a big seller. Nearly every home with daughters had a Katie Doll. So it must have something to do with what is in the house. But what is it that's in the house? And whoever lived there before us must have either something to do with it or nothing happened when the previous owners lived there.'

'Maybe we'll be lucky when we go to the library with Margaret tomorrow. And talking of tomorrow honey, maybe we should have an early night as you're up for work at six o'clock.'

Bill continued to look at the images and text on the screen, 'Hmm I'm thinking of calling Ted Mason to ask if I can start my holiday leave a week early. I've got a feeling that the problem isn't going to be sorted tonight.' Looking at his watch he noted that it was only eight fifteen and knew his boss would still be up and watching TV. Lifting his mobile to his ear he waited for an answer from the other end, 'Ted, how are you it's Bill Rodgers here. Well no, I've had an awful weekend to be honest. Listen are you free to meet up as I need to ask you something, but I need to ask you in person. I'm at the *Travel Safe Inn* on Kensington Road.

Twenty minutes later Ted Mason was knocking on the door of room 310. 'Ted please come in,' said Bill as he opened the door to allow his boss into the room. 'Sorry about all this, but when you listen to what I, we, have to tell you, I think you'll understand why I need to start my leave this week.'

Ted Mason sat down on the chair offered him and also a cup of coffee, half an hour later he sat there speechless. 'Well Ted, that's the whole story and I'll be totally honest we are scared stiff of going back into that house until we can be sure that whatever is haunting the house has been driven out.' said Bill looking grimly at his boss. 'We may even sell up and move elsewhere, that's how bad it is.'

'Would it be possible to have a small glass of that wine Bill, I think I need it after what you have just told me.' Bill passed his boss a small glass of red wine, sat down and looked at him with tired eyes.

'There is a definite connection with the doll Ted, could it be that the original owners of the doll got rid of it and over the years it has gone from one shop to another and then to the shop where eventually my sister bought it.'

'But why would a doll like the one you showed me in the photo become possessed?' asked Bill's boss quietly as he had noticed Wendy had fallen asleep on the bed and pointed at her, 'How is your daughter coping with all that's happened Bill?'

Before Bill could answer Tina said 'Maybe it would be better if you took Ted down to the bar Bill, so as not to wake Wendy up. Would that be okay Mr Mason?'

'Of course Tina and call me Ted, after all, I've known you and Bill long enough now to be on first name terms. Come on Bill let's leave the ladies to get some sleep.' Bill picked up the room door card and kissed Tina and gave her a hug, 'Kiss and a hug for our little girl too,' he said and blew a kiss at his daughter who was fast asleep.

'Do you think the paranormal team and the priest will be able to sort this thing out for you Bill?' I know I wouldn't like to be in your shoes or theirs come to think of it. All I can say Bill is yes, by all means start your holidays this week and I just hope that it is all over by tonight as you're booked to go away aren't you?' said Ted Mason as he and Bill sat in the hotel bar

Bill shook his boss's hand thanking him and ordered them both another drink from the bar before his boss left for home. 'By the way Ted, you didn't drive here did you as this is our third drink?'

'No I got my son to drive me here, he said he'll come and collect me when I'm ready to leave, and you know what Bill, even though it's a bad time for you at the moment, I'm enjoying your company as it's been a while since we had a drink together isn't it? And the good thing is I'm off tomorrow morning, hospital appointment at eleven thirty five, just a routine check-up they have told me.'

'Well in that case Ted; let's take our time, as it's good to have you to talk to about what's been going on. I'm worried about Wendy as she has had two nightmares now about the doll attacking her, and it seems to be affecting her. She's become a bit withdrawn since it all started last week, and she keeps telling us she loves us very much as if her life depended on it.'

'Keep an eye on her Bill and stay close to her at all times, both you and Tina. If what your saying is true, that you've read that spirit can attack and harm people in their dreams, then I wouldn't be too far away from her when she's sleeping.'

'Tina and I have already discussed that and we're making sure she's with us at all times at the moment. As you know Tina can't have any more children so if anything should happen to Wendy it would tear us both apart. She's our whole life Ted, and we would do anything to protect her, anything!'

Bill and Ted said their goodbyes and Bill promised to keep Ted in the loop over the next few days. Bill then made his way back to his room, brushed his teeth and used the loo as quietly as he could, changed into a t-shirt and shorts and climbed into the spare bed and watched his wife and child sleeping until finally he fell into a peaceful sleep.

.....

The two cars pulled up outside 215 Lexington Avenue and the team piled out of them both. After collecting their equipment from the trunks of the cars they made their way down the front path towards the house. Father Gabriel stopped and looked up at the attic room for a moment then continued towards the house. Inside the house all was still, the grandfather clock in the hall had stopped at three am as had all the clocks in the house. Dead time as it was known in the paranormal world.

Chapter Six

Tom Smith pushed the key into the front door lock and twisted it in the lock twice and then pushed the door open, as he did he was hit by a blast of freezing air, he shivered as he walked into the hallway followed by the others. 'Jesus it's cold in here, let's get the heating on and warm this place through.' He said as he closed the door after everyone had entered the house.

'Let's take the living room on the left this time as we don't want a repeat of what happened last time do we.'

As Joseph, Jack and Alan began to get the equipment out of the metal foam lined cases, Tom led Alexis, Jane and Father Gabriel into the smaller and comfier living room, 'Gabe would you mind sitting in here with Alexis and Jane while I give the guys a hand to set up the equipment. We're going to place most of it on the first floor landing and at the bottom of the stairs and kitchen. It's mainly camcorders that will be set up on tripods and they will be locked off so we won't need to keep monitoring them. We'll use some digital recorders too and motion detectors around the house.'

'Not a problem Tom, it'll give us chance to chat and get to know each other better, And once you've set everything up, I think it's a good idea if you all head back in here as I want to perform the opening protection prayer, similar to the one we did at your house Tom.'

Tom made his way into the hallway and up the stairs where he found the guys taking the equipment out of the cases and making sure that the camcorders were near as possible to electric sockets. The motion detectors and the other equipment worked on built in rechargeable batteries. 'Here let me take some of the motion detectors and place them in the areas that we know were active last night.' said Tom as he joined the guys on the first floor landing. As he was about to walk away with two sets of motion detectors a loud scraping sound came from the attic. All stood still and listened; it came again, sounding like something being dragged across the attic floor. Then as suddenly as it started, it stopped.

'I think whatever is up there is going to give us one hell of a night.' said Joseph, 'Come on let's get the rest of the equipment set up and get back down stairs.'

'Yes Gabe said he wants to do another protection prayer before we start and after what we have just heard, I would say that's a damn good idea.' replied Tom as he placed the second set of motion detectors at the top of the stairs, 'Let's hope these things pick up the entity's movements. Come on then guys; let's get back to the others.' As they stood in a circle in the living room, Father Gabriel recited the protection prayer and added another prayer:

'May the good lord protect us and help us tonight
And help banish the evil that is in this house
And send it into oblivion forever
Amen'

The team hugged each other then headed for the hallway, as they did the sound of motion detectors went off and the EMF meters started picking up electromagnetic changes in the atmosphere. 'It's starting to build its energy up again, be ready and be strong everyone.' shouted Joseph, 'let's get up the stairs now!' As they ran up the stairs they noticed the air had gone ice cold again even though the heating was on all over the house. As they neared the attic room the dragging sound came again, 'My god it sounds like its moving furniture around up there.' cried Alexis

Now standing in front of the attic, Father Gabriel said, 'I think it's time that we faced this evil, don't you. Have any of you been up here yet?' All shook their heads in response. 'Well it's now or never, so let's do this!' The priest pulled open the door, walking over the threshold he reached in to his inside jacket pocket and pulled out his crucifix and held it up in the air and began to walk up the attic steps, and as he did, the attic door slammed shut, the priest turned round and tried to turned the doorknob and tried to push it open, it wouldn't budge. 'Hey guys, get the door open again, we all need to be in here!' the priest shouted loudly. Outside Tom twisted the door handle and then yelled in pain, 'Shit its red hot! How are we going to open it now?'

Alan turned around and made for the stairs, I'll see if there is an axe somewhere, the family must have one as they have log burners and a stack of logs ready for chopping outside.

Inside the attic Father Gabriel could hear movement and what sounded like a male voice which appeared to be inside his head, 'So priest, are you the same as all the other priests, believing in witchcraft and hanging people for their own beliefs?' Father Gabriel knew he had to be strong and began to walk up the steps and stood in the attic. He reached into his right hand jacket pocket and pulled out a torch, switching it on he scanned the attic to look for the source of the voice. 'Show yourself to me!' Gabriel shouted. There was nothing in the room, even the doll had vanished from there. He then heard loud banging coming from the attic door and realised that Tom or one of the guys must have found an axe and were trying their best to smash the door open.

As Tom was wielding the axe and making a fair sized hole in the door, Jane and Alexis stood by the top of the stairs, suddenly Jane let out an almighty scream, all looked in her direction and then to where she was pointing in fear. Coming up the stairs was the doll, slowly taking each step one at a time, stopping in the middle of the stairs for moment, then continued upwards. As it reached the top, Alexis pushed Jane out of the way and the swung her leg back and kicked the doll as hard as she could. The doll flew through the air and landed in a heap down by the front door, 'That should keep her quiet for a while!' cried Alexis and apologised to Jane for pushing her out the way. Jane just smiled and hugged her friend, 'Thanks babe, I froze there sorry.'

Tom had virtually smashed the door to pieces by now and they were all able to get up into the attic. As the team got into the room they found Father Gabriel looking out of the attic window, Joseph walked over to him and tapped him on the shoulder, 'Hey Gabe are you alright?' Slowly the priest turned around and said, 'I think I have just heard its voice, it was in my head. It asked me if I believed in witchcraft and hanging people. I think we need to say a prayer up here.

The the team joined in with the prayer and splashing holy water around the room. 'Let's go downstairs into the living room, and let's make sure that the doll is still where it landed before. If it is, hack it to pieces with the axe and then we'll burn it!'

'Dear God do you think it's over Joseph?' asked Jack as they all sat in the living room

'No Jack, I don't, I think this is only the beginning, the atmosphere in the attic is still chilled. We need to discuss what to do next while it's quiet.'

Father Gabriel sat nursing a whiskey and appeared deep in thought after his experience. 'I'm baffled as to why the spirit, which I believe it was, asked me that kind of question. It didn't sound evil, just angry.'

'What do you mean Gabe?' asked Jack as he too nursed a glass of whiskey.

'This is just the beginning of the fight; the entity has shown us what it is capable of by trapping one of us, namely me. Has anyone seen the doll as it wasn't in the attic?' asked the priest

It was downstairs all the time Gabe, it began walking on its own accord up the stairs and Alexis kicked it back down. Tom asked us to chop it up and then we were going to burn it?' replied Jane.

'You said going to burn it, where is it?'

'That's the thing, while we were all in the attic it must have got up and now it could be anywhere in the house!' replied Jane.

'I'm afraid we're going to be here sometime, this is not going to be an easy victory, and in fact it may end up being extremely dangerous as we have already seen.' Father Gabriel said as he finished off his whiskey. 'I think we should leave the house shortly, leave all the equipment running while we are away. But take the tapes out of the camcorders so we can view them somewhere safe, and put new ones in. Tom, are we okay to all go back to your house for a rest and maybe view some of the footage?'

'Of course you can, you're all welcome to stay as long as you want while we're dealing with this problem. I'm on leave now for two weeks and Alan has a week, so we'll be able to carry on for as long as necessary.'

'In that case everyone' while it is quiet, let's get the tapes out of the machines and get the hell out of here. I for one have had enough for one night.' replied Father Gabriel. As they left the room and entered the hallway, they were all confronted by the doll, it stood looking at them all, its arms were twisted from the fall and its lower face was cracked where Alexis had kicked it. Tom rushed over to the front door and picked up the axe where Alexis had left it. With all his might he swung the axe and with a loud swishing sound swung the axe and decapitated the doll. Picking the head and body up he shouted, 'Quick outside we need to burn this doll now!'

The team went outside into the back garden and found a metal bin which had the remnants of a fire inside it. Dropping the head and body into the bin, Tom asked if anyone had a lighter, Father Gabriel pulled one out of his pocket, 'I don't smoke but I always carry a lighter in my pocket. He flicked the lighter and held the flame to the remnants of the dolls black dress and then to its long black hair. All stood watching it burn and then Father Gabriel said a prayer over it and as the flames licked and consumed the doll he splashed holy water over it, which made the flames burn brighter for a few seconds. After retrieving the video tapes they needed they all left the house and securely locking all exits, climbed into the two cars and made their way to Tom's house on High Cross Lane.

It was at this point that Wendy threw the bed covers off herself and started moaning in her sleep and began tossing and turning as if she was having a bad dream. Suddenly she sat up straight in the bed and screamed out loud 'They're burning me, they're burning me!' and then fell back on the bed and continued sleeping. Bill switched on the light and looked over to the double bed where his wife and daughter lay, his daughter was sound asleep, but his wife had also been woken up by their daughter's frantic yelling. Both looked at each other and then at their sleeping daughter. They would talk to her in the morning about what had happened and if she remembered anything.

Chapter Seven

As the Rodgers family prepared to go down for breakfast at the hotel, so too were Tom Smith and his guests at his house on High Cross Lane. The Rodgers were now deeply concerned about their daughter and the latest incident to occur the night before. As Bill took a shower Tina sat brushing Wendy's hair which she had always liked as it chilled her out. 'Wendy love, did you have another bad dream last night?'

'I can't remember mum, why are you asking, did something happen?' asked Wendy.

'Well at one point in the night you sat up in bed shouting, 'they're burning me, they're burning me!', and it woke me and your dad up. We're so worried about you chicken.' replied Tina as she gave her daughter a loving hug.

Bill had finished in the shower and walked in to the room, 'Hey how are my two favourite ladies in the whole world today?' Bill walked over to his wife and daughter and kissed them both, 'I love you too so much and I promise with all my heart that we are going to be back home very soon and then we can go away on our holidays as planned.'

In the house on High Cross Lane, Tom Smith had been joined in the kitchen by Alexis and she offered to help him cook breakfast for everyone and lay the table as well. The table was a huge old farmhouse table which Tom had bought at an auction along with eight rustic chairs, it looked splendid in the long dining room which Tom had built on to the back of the kitchen years earlier. Alexis found the drawer with the utensils in and started to lay seven places. She found a stack of place mats and arranged the table as if fit for a king, 'Hey Tom I spotted some nice flowers out front in your garden, is it okay to get some for the table?'

'Why sure Alexis by all means.' replied Tom busy turning over the sausages and bacon on the large grill. He had eggs frying in a large frying pan and a pan full of beans. He had the oven on low to keep the plates warm and to place the cooked eggs as well when they were ready. Next he placed slices of black pudding into the frying pan and kept an eye on them so as not to overcook them.

Alexis came back into the kitchen and asked if Tom had such a thing as a vase. Tom said there should be one in the cupboard to the left of where she was standing. She found it and half filled it with water, then she arranged the flowers and placed them in the middle of the table. As she stood looking at her handy work the sun shone through a tall window and lit her features and body up. Tom felt his heart skip a beat as he looked at her. 'Hey Miss Bishop you have done a splendid job there, very professional indeed.'

'Good to know I've not lost the knack of laying tables Mr Smith.' she replied with a big smile on her face. 'I used to work in a posh hotel in Kensington, London as a waitress and had to learn the correct way in laying and waiting on tables, so it's come in handy in later life I'd say ha ha.'

Tom kept looking at her and said, 'would you mind if I took a photo of you exactly where you are standing Alexis?'

Alexis looked surprised, 'Why Mr Smith I didn't know you cared, of course if you want to you can.' Tom pulled his mobile phone out of his pocket and made sure the light on her was perfect, then took about four photos of Alexis. When he had finished she walked over to Tom and asked to see the photos he'd just taken. 'Hey I can see why you wanted to take a pic of me, the sun shining down and the shadows are perfect.'

'You're perfect Alexis, perfect in every way.' replied Tom, they looked at each other and then into each other's eyes, 'So are you Tom, I've been finding it hard to keep my eyes off you since I met you the other night, which seems so long ago now doesn't it.' replied Alexis as she put her arms around Tom's waist and then kissed him softly on the lips, 'that's just for starters honey, now let's not let this wonderful breakfast you're cooking get burnt to a crisp. Both Tom and Alexis took control of cooking the breakfast and as they did they could hear footsteps above them, 'hmm sounds like your guests are getting ready to come down, they must have spelt the cooking.' Alexis said as she stirred the pan full of beans and then went to fill the kettle up to make pots of tea to go with the breakfast.

......

Sitting in the dining room of the hotel, Bill and Tina asked Wendy again if she could remember anything about her dreams last night, but Wendy said she couldn't. Tina heard her phone ringing and took it out of the back pocket of her jeans, 'Hi Margaret, how are you? Lovely to hear from you after so long, Yes Bill's told me that you're coming into Coldport today to research our house and who lived there. Yes we'd love to help and the good news is we've got an extra pair of eyes as Bill has been allowed to start his holidays this week. Yes meet us at the hotel, you remember where it is? Okay we'll see you in forty five minutes, bye for now.' Tina put the phone back into her back pocket. 'Let's hope we get to the bottom of the problem now Bill.'

Bill finished his breakfast and looked pensive, 'I wonder how Tom Smith and the team got on last night? I hope they were successful.' He looked at his phone and thought about ringing Tom to ask him, but then thought better of it. 'I was going to phone Tom, but if they were up all night I reckon they will still be asleep.'

Tina took hold of Bill's hand and caressed it, 'Honey, I'm sure Tom will call you, he said he would, and remember his promise to our little girl here. Come on, let's go and get ourselves ready for Margaret's arrival. Hey chicken are you okay, you look like you're going to fall asleep there.' Tina kissed Wendy on the head and the family left the dining room and headed for their room.

·····

Everyone sat around the old farmhouse table in Tom's dining room and ate heartily and chatted about different things, all trying to avoid what happened last night, but knowing they would have to broach the subject sooner or later. Tom and Alexis sat next to each other and seemed to be getting closer as they chatted and giggled a lot, which didn't go unnoticed by the others. 'Well at least something good has come out of us all meeting this weekend.' said Jane smiling and looking at the happy couple, everyone laughed and smiled at Tom and Alexis and both of them blushed like a young couple in love for the first time.

'Well I think it's time that we talked about what has happened over the weekend.' said Joseph as he refilled his cup from the second pot of tea.

Once all the dishes and cutlery were placed into the dish washer Tom and Alexis joined everyone else in the living room, 'Does anybody want to start or do you want me to?' asked Joseph as he sat in one of the armchairs. 'Go ahead Joe, and let's see what plan we can come up with as up to know we've not been successful except for hacking up and burning the doll.' said Jack as he sipped from his now warm tea.

'Well, I think now that we have got rid of that horrible doll, we will only have to concentrate on the dark entity, which I prefer to call it, a demon seems to conjure up the devil in my mind. Anyway, we now know that it can trap not only us but Father Gabriel as well. We have got to stay together and not get separated again. And now that the attic door has been virtually demolished it can't separate us up there. And I think you would all agree with me that the dark entity is bound to that area, why it is, is anyone's guess.'

Everyone nodded in agreement, 'Well I say that we should go back tonight and finish this off once and for all!' said Alexis, 'have we any news yet from the family Tom about the house and the doll?'

'Not yet, but I know that they were meeting up with Bill's sister Margaret, the lady who bought the doll for Bill's daughter. They are going to…' Tom's mobile phone rang and he looked at who was calling, 'Hey Bill how are you guys coping? We were just discussing the case here at my house. I'm afraid all we've managed to do is to get rid of the doll; we chopped her head off and set fire to her in your metal bin in the garden. At what time, why do you ask Bill?' Bill Rodgers explained that during the night Wendy had sat up in bed, totally asleep and shouted out, 'They're burning me' twice then fell back to sleep, but she had no recollection of it at all this morning.

'I don't like the sound of this Bill, it sounds like there is a connection between the doll and Wendy, but what?' Please let me know as soon as you find anything at the library as we need all the information we can get. If you do find anything do you think you'll be able to send it over to me via email, providing you can find anything out that is?' Tom gave Bill his email address and wished him luck.

Everyone looked at Tom after he ended the call and asked what happened to Bill's daughter. Tom explained what Bill had said and then said, 'All we can do is wait and see if they can find anything out about the house. He said that they had found out that the doll was a very popular doll called Katie in the Victorian era and nearly every household with little girls had a *Katie Doll*, so it can't be the doll that was evil, it has been manipulated by the dark entity all along.'

They all decided that they would wait for any information to come through before they planned their next investigation of the house. So it was decided that they would spend the next couple of hours going through the video tapes from the night before. What interested them the most were two things; one was the entity outside the attic, which appeared to be the height and build of a male. The second and most compelling was the doll walking up the staircase. The camcorder placed at the bottom of the stairs had captured it perfectly, it captured a dark smaller shape like that of a child, a appeared to be manipulating the doll. After discussing the footage and replaying it countless times, Tom suggested that they all take a break for a few hours and do something else to take their minds off things. Jack and Jane headed off home so that they could freshen up and change clothes and sort out any business they needed to take care of. Father Gabriel, who had been very quiet most of the morning, headed back to his apartment and was then going to have a word with the Bishop regarding the house and what had happened to him in the attic. Joseph went back home for a few hours as did Alan. Once everyone had left Tom's house Tom and Alexis decided to take a walk on the beach.

.....

In the library Bill and his family had been directed to the archives section and began scouring old newspapers dating back to the early 1800's. Margaret was looking through old house records and located a section regarding the houses on Lexington Avenue in Coldport. As she read she was amazed at what she read, she called Bill over to the table where she had the book open. 'Bill look at this I've found, it says that prior to your house being built there was an older house which dates back to the days of Cromwell, the late 1500's or there about. It also says that the house was extended a number of times over the years as larger families lived in the house. Now let's see if we can get some information on who actually lived there from when it was first built.'

At that moment Tina and Wendy walked over to where Bill and his sister were sitting. 'We've come across a book which I think will be very interesting indeed.' said Tina placing the book down on the table. The book was called *The History of Coldport and its Families*, which was bound in leather and had two leather straps with buckles on it. The text was all handwritten and traced the history of families and properties and was a consummate book about Coldport. Tina looked through the contents list which was twenty pages long, 'Ah here we are, Lexington Avenue properties and who owned them, page two hundred and five!' Tina found the section they were after, 'Now then let's see, here we are, 215 Lexington Avenue, originally called Seaport Lane.

1643 to 1645 the house, a small cottage was built by Mr and Mrs Bartholomew who lived there with their only child, a girl. Rumour has it that in 1645 the Bartholomew's were accused of witchcraft and it was Matthew Hopkins, the Witchfinder General who accused them of heresy and the family were forced to confess to being witches, even their twelve year old daughter. They were all hung on Gallows Hill which was a mile from their cottage.

In 1648 Mr Edmund Butterworth bought the land and knocked down the derelict cottage and built a large house for his wife and daughter and son, the house was a single fronted house but boasted a large living room, kitchen, basement and three bedrooms. Apparently Mr Butterworth was quite a rich man for the time. It is said that his family were well liked and respected and at one time Edmund Butterworth worked for Cromwell.

From 1668 to 1888, it is stated that the house had at least ten different families living there. Three of the families had one child, a girl, and they never stayed longer than a year. Seven families had large families and it was a Mr and Mrs Abraham Donleavy that added the final part of the house in 1868, extending it upwards to include a large attic, and an extra bedroom was added as was a second living room.

The house fell into disrepair after the Donleavy's left the house for reasons unknown.

1971 to 1999, the house has four more occupiers all of whom never stayed long for reasons unknown and again the four couples only had one child, a girl.

2000 to 2010 the house was empty for most part and it says here that the house got the nickname of 'The Devil's House' as screams and loud banging noises would emanate from the house even though it was empty!

'And now, as dated 2015, according to the book it says we are the new owners, so it must get updated whenever someone moves in or moves out judging by the change in handwriting over the years.' finished of Tina.

'Don't you find it strange that families never stayed in the house very long, and a lot of them only had one child and each time it was a girl?' remarked Margaret and she turned some of the pages back. 'I hate to point this out but the Bartholomew family that were hung for being witches could have put a hex on the town or on the house. Also, you have never mentioned the basement Bill, why is that.'

'Because I didn't know until now that there was a basement in the house, and we've never found an entrance to it.' replied Bill.

'Have you found any strange markings in the attic space, or on the floors of the other rooms? By strange I mean pentagrams drawn in chalk, they may be anywhere in the house Bill?'

'No none at all, the few times we've been in the attic we've not seen any all, and we recovered all the floors in every room with new carpets, so I'm sure we would have come across something like a pentagram if there was one.'

'I truly believe the problem stems from the Bartholomew family, as we now know, the *Katie Doll* was very popular so we can't blame the Donleavy family for that problem can we?'

'But how on earth did the *Katie Doll* get to the shop in Boxley after all those years?' asked Tina. Looking at her daughter she noticed she looked bored. 'Hey chicken, do you wanna go see if we can find an ice cream van and stuff ourselves with ice cream and take a walk along the beach?' Wendy smiled at her mum, 'that would be great mum, can we have some chips too as I'm hungry?'

Tina gave Bill a kiss and hugged Margaret, 'I think my little girl needs to get some fresh air, I know I do. You don't mind us leaving you to it for an hour do you?' Both Bill and his sister said they didn't mind at all and gave Wendy a big hug, then continued to go through more documents.

'I'm going to see if it's okay to scan the pages out of this book and then save them to my phone and some of the photos too.' Said Bill as he picked up the old leather bound book.

'If you scan the pages of the book Bill I'll scan the photos, we can then send both lots via email to Sergeant Smith straight away can't we?' replied Margaret picking up a handful of old sepia photos of how the house looked like over the years.

.....

Tom and Alexis sat in a café sipping tea and chatting to each other and finding out what each other's likes and dislikes were. 'So what's made you want to retire Tom, you're too young aren't you?' Alexis asked placing her cup back on the table.

'Well seeing as how you've asked my sweet lady, I feel that nearly twenty years in law enforcement is enough for anyone and too be honest I feel it's time to settle down with someone again.' replied Tom as he finished drinking his tea.

'Hmm, so you've been in a relationship before, what happened?'

'Yes I have, I was married with two kids, Tommy and Angela, my wife's name was Lorraine, here's photo of them.' said Tom opening his wallet and taking a photo out.

'They look lovely Tom, what happened, did you get divorced?'

'No Alexis, my wife and two kids were killed in a car smash, a drunk driver ploughed into them, and they were all killed outright. He got five years, that's all, five years. But thank god he's dead now. He became an addict and one day someone pumped him full of dirty cocaine. We never found out whom, but I would have shaken the hand of the person who did.'

'Oh Tom, I'm so sorry, I shouldn't have pried into your private life like that.' Alexis took hold of Tom's hand, 'If it's too soon for you to have a relationship with me, I'll totally understand.'

'It's okay Alexis, the accident happened ten years ago and all this time, I've had to hold things together on my own, but now I feel it is time to move on and I think you are the right person to help me move on with my life. That's if you want too?'

The couple smiled at each other and got up to leave, Tom went and paid for the teas and they left the café hand in hand. 'I've told you that I want to become a full time paranormal investigator haven't I honey?' Alexis nodded as they walked along the warm sands of Coldport beach, they had taken their shoes and socks off and walked barefoot, letting the warm sand slip through their toes. 'Well I would like the two of us to team up together and hold investigations. Maybe get the help of Joe and Gabe now and again if we needed them, what do you say?' Alexis stopped walking as did Tom and she kissed him softly, 'If it means me spending more time with you Tom, then I would say yes I would love to investigate hauntings with you.' They kissed again and then began walking. As they did, Bill's mobile phone rang, 'Hi Tom Smith speaking, Bill, good to hear from you, have you found anything out yet?'

'We have Tom, and I've sent you some very interesting documents and my sister has sent you old photos of the house through different eras. I think we now know where the problem lies in the house, but you may need to go searching for something in there first. Apparently there is supposed to be a basement in the house which may or may not have a pentagram drawn on the floor of it.'

Tom ended the call and let Alexis now what Tom had said, 'Come on we need to get back to my house and check my emails. I think we'll need to get the rest of the guys back as soon as possible too.'

Back at his house Tom, turned on his laptop and connected it to a printer, finding the two emails sent to him as promised, he opened them and clicked on the attachments, once opened he clicked print and waited for the first attachment to print off. He did the same with the second attachment, and then both he and Alexis sat on the sofa and together went through the document and the photos. 'Now we know where the trouble has arisen from, the family that were hung as witches. They must have placed a curse on the house or on the town, but it looks more and more like it could be the three members of the family that are haunting the house, wouldn't you say Alexis?'

Alexis studied the old photos of the house and was drawn to the kitchen area in each photo. 'I agree Tom and I think the basement is somewhere in the kitchen, I'm drawn to that area in each photo.'

As they continued studying the photos and documents a knock came to the front door. Tom rose out of the sofa and headed into the hallway, upon opening the door, he was confronted by Joseph, Alan and Jack and Jane, 'Come in one and all. We have got some pretty good, no, excellent information from Bill Rodgers regarding his house. But where's Father Gabriel?'

'He's going to be a bit late as he's in talks with his Bishop regarding what went on last night. He feels we are going to need a lot more protection when we return tonight.' replied Joseph as he walked over to where Alexis was sitting. 'So what have we got here?'

Tom handed the printed off documents to the team and headed into the kitchen to make them all a cup of tea. On his return he noticed the look of concern on Joseph's face. 'What's the matter Joe, have you spotted something Alexis and I haven't?'

'No Tom I'm just even more concerned about Wendy now, with what you told us about her waking up last night at the exact time we burnt the doll shouting 'They're burning me! Could it be the spirit of the Bartholomew's daughter that is the connection and it is her spirit that has inhabited the doll all this time?'

'You mean it might be the daughter's spirit manipulating the doll to make it move like we saw in the video footage earlier, and her parents are the ones in the attic?' asked Jane

'I feel as if that is what we're up against in that house. What else did Bill Rodgers tell you Tom?' asked Alan Davies.

'He said that that if you read the notes you will notice that when the house was constructed in 1648 they had a basement. Now Bill says he has never known about a basement in the house, and more to the point, we haven't noticed one either have we?' replied Tom.

'That's right we haven't! So we need to find the basement especially if the Bartholomew family were tried as witches, they may have practiced black magic in the basement. We need to find it and now! I say let's get round there now while it's daylight and look for any hidden doors in all the ground floor rooms.' replied Joseph.

Finishing their cups of tea the team decided that they would go back to the house straight away. Tom went into his garage and brought out two crowbars, 'I've got a feeling we'll need these guys.'

Margaret Rodgers had invited the family to leave the hotel and stay at her house in Boxley. Her house had three bedrooms and a large kitchen and living room, so there would be plenty of room for them all to stay. 'It's going to cost you a fortune if you stay in the hotel any longer, so I won't take no for an answer Bill.' The four of them walked back down Kensington Road to the hotel and went to their room to collect their belongings. Back down at the reception desk Bill paid for the room with his credit card and leaving the hotel they got into their cars and drove to Margaret's house.

Margaret showed them their rooms and told them to make themselves at home and relax. 'Now that you're out of the town just try and relax and leave the problem to the team of investigators, I'll go and pop the kettle on and make some sandwiches, come down when you're ready.'

'This is so nice of Margaret isn't it Bill, I just hope she still doesn't feel like she's the one that caused the problem with buying the doll in the first place.' said Tina as she began to unpack the few clothes they had with them.

Bill walked over to his wife and held her close to him, 'Do you know something, I love you so much. With all that is happening at the moment, you haven't panicked or shown any fear at all. You're a very brave lady indeed.'

Tina kissed Bill and looked at him, 'I have to be Bill, for Wendy's sake, we both have to be. I'm really worried about her, she's so quiet. When we went for the walk on the beach earlier, she hardly said a word, and you know what a chatterbox she can be.'

Bill kissed his wife again, 'We'll keep a close eye on her and make sure nothing happens to her. I'm sure once this is all over, she will be back to her normal chatty happy self.'

The family gathered in Margaret's living room and chatted while having the snack Margaret had prepared for them and all seemed to relax at long last.

.....

'Excuse me your Grace, I just need to take this call, it's Joseph Daniels, I won't be long.' Father Gabriel stood up and left the room and stood in the corridor of the Bishop's residence, 'Joseph how are you?' Joseph told Father Gabriel that they were outside 215 Lexington Avenue at that very moment. He told him about the listing of owners and photos that the Rodgers family had gathered from the Coldport library.

'And you are going to try and find the entrance to the basement now? I'm going to ask His Grace if Father Driscoll can help us, as I feel we are going to need his help too.'

Father Gabriel went back into the Bishop's office and informed him of what had happened. 'Would it be possible to have Father Driscoll accompany me to the house and help me?'

'Of course Father Gabriel, I'll ring for him now.' The Bishop dialled a number and it was answered straight away. He briefly explained what the problem was and five minutes later, Father Driscoll was standing alongside Father Gabriel. The two priests shook hands and Father Gabriel said he would explain in detail the ordeal the Rodgers family have been going through as well as the paranormal investigators, him and the two policemen while he drove them to the Rodgers house.

'What, the police are involved as well, my god, how come they are involved Gabe?' asked Father Jeff Driscoll.

Sergeant Tom Smith received a call from Bill Rodgers on Friday night as they thought they had an intruder in the attic room of the house. He turned up with three officers and when they went up to the attic all hell broke loose, but it wasn't a human intruder, it was something paranormal and one of the officers was attacked...by a doll!' Father Gabriel then went on to tell the wide eyed priest sitting in the passenger seat next to him everything that had happened since Friday night. 'So now we need to find this basement and what is in it as it could be the catalyst for what is going on.'

.....

Wendy lay asleep on the large comfy armchair and the family looked once again at the information that they had printed off for themselves as well as for the police sergeant. Bill kept going over the names and details of the extensions added to the house since its first construction. Bill was convinced that the basement had to be either under the grand staircase, or in the kitchen, and if it was, it was very well hidden. 'I think the entrance has been boarded up for a reason, and for one reason only, the dark entity has been haunting the house since the Bartholomew's lived there. I think, but I could be totally wrong in my way of thinking, but I think the house is haunted by all three members of that family!'

Chapter Eight

As Father Gabriel drove up Lexington Avenue he started to feel a deep sense of dread and horror and took a quick glance at Father Driscoll and knew that he was feeling the same as he was. He slowed the car down and pulled over to the left hand side of the road. Switching the engine off he turned to his colleague and asked if he was ready to do what they had come to do. Father Driscoll nodded and the two priests' climbed out of the vehicle and headed towards the two cars in front of them. On seeing the two priests walking towards the parked cars, Joe, Jack, Jane, Alexis, Tom and Alan piled out of their cars. After introductions and handshakes all round everybody grabbed all the equipment and holy items they needed which were all in flight cases, except the two priests, they both had leather cases that looked like old doctors bags. Tom and Alan both grabbed a large sledgehammer and a crowbar each. As they all neared the house the feeling of dread was mounting and they all knew that they were being watched by something unseen, something evil.

Tom dropped the sledgehammer and crowbar to the floor and fished inside his jacket pocket for the house key. Twisting it in the lock twice he turned the ornate door knob and pushed the door wide open and everyone walked inside. Collecting his tools Tom also walked inside and closed the door behind him. Even in the daytime the house felt dark, oppressive and evil. 'Let's take the living room on the left again everybody and once we are ready, find that basement.' said Tom.

Tom had spent some time earlier drawing a ground floor plan of the house by memory and with the help of some of the photos that Margaret had sent him via email. He had also done a rough plan of the first floor, and attic, from his brief but harrowing time in there. 'Okay everyone I've done some rough plans of both floors and their rooms,' opening them up and laying them on a large oak table he continued, 'I think the area under the stairs and the kitchen could be the best places to start looking. I only say this as the paranormal events that have occurred have been on the stairs and in the kitchen.' Looking at Jane he asked if she would be okay going back in the kitchen, Jane nodded saying as long as everyone was with her she would be fine and with the doll being destroyed she felt better.

'Right folks let's try under the staircase first.' As they walked towards the door they all gave a curious look up the stairs, all appeared quiet. The team split into two and began knocking on the walls either side of the grand staircase.

'Here we are I think I've found something!' shouted Father Driscoll. On the left hand side of the staircase part of the wall sounded false.

'It could be the doorway we're looking for.' replied Joseph. 'Let's get the sledgehammer on it!' After pounding a hole in the plasterboard they managed to find what appeared to be an entranceway, but the walls inside were solid. 'Oh well let's try the kitchen.'

They all walked together into the right hand side living room and then through the archway and short passageway leading to the kitchen. Again they banged and knocked on all the walls and were totally mystified as all the walls were solid. 'Damn, the entrance must be in here surely!' shouted Joseph hurting his right hand as he banged a wall in frustration.

'Hey Joe are you alright that was some whack you took there?' asked Alexis as she took a look at his hand. 'Yeah fine Alexis thanks, just frustrated. Hey do you have your crystal pendulum with you?' Alexis nodded and produced a five sided crystal which ended in a point and was attached to a silver chain.

'What's the idea Joe, we're looking for an entrance to a basement not buried treasure.' joked Alan Davies.

'Alexis is one of the best dowsers I know, even though she doesn't boast about it. The idea is for Alexis to ask questions and use the pendulum to locate the entrance. You have to see it to believe it; do you want to try it out Alexis?' Alexis nodded and began to concentrate asking the pendulum to show her 'Yes' which it did by moving in a clockwise motion, when she asked for 'No' it swung back and forth.

'Can you show me where the basement is please?' nothing.

'Please direct me to the entrance of the basement.' The crystal began to move back and forth and then it stopped abruptly and then began to move clockwise, as it did it spun faster and faster and without warning it stopped in a straight line and the crystal was pointing to a large Welsh dresser in one of the kitchen's large alcoves. 'It's there behind the dresser, I've convinced the way it stopped straight in the air pointing in that area.' cried Alexis as she pocketed the now warm and still crystal. Everyone started taking all the plates and pots off the dresser and then tried to move it.

'Damn it weighs a ton, let's take the drawers out as well, it should make it lighter and easier to move.' Alan said as he began pulling out the first of three drawers below the shelving. The dresser moved easier with four of the men lifting it. They placed it along a wall further down the kitchen and then walked back to the space. Tom knocked on the wall, 'By god it sounds hollow.' Grabbing a sledgehammer he swung it in an arc and hit the wall. After the second and third time he began to make a hole large enough to peer into. He saw a corridor which was about eight foot in length and covered in cobwebs. Tom reached into the back pocket of his jeans and pulled put a small but strong Maglite torch. Shining the beam through the gaping hole, he could see an old door, 'I think we have just located the door to the basement folks.' He said turning around and smiling and then gave Alexis a big hug, 'You kept that quiet about you powers with the crystal pendulum honey, but I'm so happy that you used your talents to locate the entrance.'

The rest of the wall came down easily with both Tom and Alan hammering at it; and soon it was large enough for everyone to walk through. As they stood brushing dust off of themselves, Joseph stood listening to something, and then he looked upwards. 'I think we may have company upstairs listen.' They all listened and Tom picked up one of the crowbars. 'That sounds like someone walking along the landing, you don't think someone has broken in and are hiding do you?' asked Jane.

'I don't think anyone would be stupid enough to after what the neighbours heard the other night do you Jane. But I agree, it does sound like footsteps up there. Alan let's take a look and see what it is.' said Tom and he began to move through the kitchen with his colleague. Two minutes later they heard the two men yell and the sound of them running back to the kitchen, 'You are not going to believe this, it's the bloody doll, standing at the top of the stairs, all back together but blackened from the fire!'

The rest of the team stood in shock and were totally lost for words; Tom reacted first my grabbing a sledgehammer and told Alan to do the same. 'We are going to smash that bloody doll to pieces, every single part of it. And hopefully that will stop some of the activity!' The two men rushed out the hallway and saw the doll now standing near the entrance under the stairs, 'Ready mate let's do this!'

Ten minutes later the two policemen stopped and dropped the large hammers to the floor. The doll, what was left of it, was unrecognisable, smashed to a pulp. They swept it into a waste bin and took it outside a burn it. As they did this both priests said prayers over it and then sprinkled holy water over it. They then piled four heavy logs onto the dolls remains and watched as the flames licked the logs as well as the doll. She wouldn't get out a second time.

Back in the house they returned to the entrance to the basement, Jane used the sweeping brush to clear the years of cobwebs as they were so thick, and as she did spiders of various sizes scuttled around looking for a way out. Tom handed Joseph a crowbar and said as he was a demonologist and real life investigator, he could have the pleasure of prying open the old door. 'Sure thing Tom, here goes everyone, be on your guard at all times as we don't know what could be inside.' Joseph placed the crowbar into the side of the door near the lock and with an almighty push the door flew open. They were all hit by the smell of decay making them gag.

'Jesus, sorry Father's that smells like death doesn't it?' said Jack holding his sleeve to his nose to block out the smell. 'It could be dead rats or mice that have been trapped in there.'

'I think we should go in first everyone, Father Driscoll are you ready, right let's see what is smelling so bad in there.' As they walked in both priests began coughing, Father Gabriel turned his torch on and shone the beam around the basement room. 'There appears to be a number of rooms in here, but no bodies of rats or anything else for that matter. Tom and Alan walked into the basement, which was massive, it must have been the length and breadth of the whole house and as Father Gabriel noted had three doorways to the right as they entered. 'Oh hell you're right Gabe, sorry Father Gabriel, I wonder what the hell is in here making that smell. And I wonder what could be behind those doors.'

'Only one way to find out Tom,' said Alan, 'let's see what secrets they hold.' both men walked over to the doors and tried the handles, 'Well they're unlocked anyway.' After checking all the rooms all they found was piles of old furniture and a large wine rack which still held around thirty to forty bottles of wine. 'So where is the stench coming from? It's not the smell of fresh decay, but seems to be old and has been hanging in the unopened basement forever. So what are we looking for in here anyway Tom?'

Moving around the room Tom said 'I think we'll know when we find it Alan. Let's regroup up in the living room; mind you after being in here I could do with some fresh air now.'

Closing the basement door as best they could they all hurried back to the front door to get some fresh air but it would not open, 'Damn not again, let's try the back door,' that too was locked tight by some unknown force.

'Right only one way out of this house.' said Tom picking up the sledgehammer and striking the back door. It didn't even make a mark on it. 'Well I'll be, what kind of force are these spirits using here?'

'Hang on and let's not panic, let's do what we did the first night we were all here when Alan came with back up. You just opened the front door didn't you Alan?' said Joseph.

'Yes, I'll call the station now and ask for back up again.' said Alan.

This time it was Superintendent Fisher who arrived this time, and turning the door knob walked into the hallway. Tom appeared from the living room along with everyone else, 'that door was locked sir we couldn't get out like last time, how weird. We've found the basement sir and there appears to be something decaying in there but we don't know what or where about in there.'

'Okay let's get down to the basement, by the way Tom where is it? It looks like you've been having a renovation party in here, looking for the basement I imagine.' Tom led the way through the living room on the right along the short passageway and once in the kitchen he pointed at the old corridor leading to it.

'There are three more rooms in there sir, but all are just filled with old furniture and a large wine rack. We can't locate the smell, whatever it is.' replied Tom as they walked into the basement. Tom, Alan and their boss walked around the basement and again looked in the three rooms finding nothing to be causing the smell which was now becoming stronger in one area of the basement. As they stood next to the far wall opposite the wall with the three rooms, they all noticed that the smell was a lot stronger there, but still found nothing to indicate where it was coming from.

Chapter Nine

'Tom, is there any decent whiskey or brandy in the house? I sure could do with one right now, I can taste the decay in my mouth, yuk!' asked Fisher. Tom lead the way to the living room on the left of the house, knowing it housed a drinks cabinet. As they walked into the room everyone was chatting and having a drink. Pulling open the drinks cabinet Tom poured his boss a large brandy, 'There you are sir, that should help get rid of the foul taste in your throat, I know I need one, Alan, the same for you mate?' his colleague nodded

'So did you guys find the cause of the smell down there?' asked Joseph.

'No we didn't but I still feel we're missing something. I can't understand why there is a blocked off area under the stairs, unless it was another way into the basement?' said Alan Davies, now sitting down alongside Joseph Daniels.

Joseph got up and walked around the room and appeared to be deep in thought, 'I've got it guys, that's it! It all makes sense now. Well I hope it does.'

'What are you on about Joseph' asked Father Gabriel as he finished off his whiskey and walked back over to the drinks cabinet and poured himself another shot. 'Does anyone else want a refill?' all said yes and the priest refilled all the glasses with whiskeys and brandies.

The demonologist looked at everyone in the room, 'Right what have we found up to now, a family that lived in a cottage on this site in the 1600's who were tried and hung as witches. The cottage was demolished and a new house was built on the plot. None of the other families who lived in the house stayed very long as we found out from the records Bill Rodgers sent to Tom a few days ago. Now, here is the crux of the problem. We know that the family that lived in the house, when it was smaller of course, were a father, mother and daughter that were all hung as witches as we're led to believe from ancient records. We also know that a lot of the families that didn't stay long consisted of husband, wife and daughter.' Daniels paused to take a large gulp of whiskey and found that he had finished it; Father Gabriel refilled the glass for him.

Placing his glass down on a small side table next to him the demonologist continued with his hypothesis, 'We also know from the old records that the area used to be called, 'Gallows Hill', it all makes perfect sense.'

Superintendent Fisher was the first to comment, 'I hate to sound thick Mr Daniels, but what makes perfect sense, I don't quite follow?'

'I think I know what Joe is getting at sir, said Tom, 'Four families of three, possibly all the children were girls, all have been so frightened over the years that they just upped and left. Maybe, just maybe...'

'You're thinking along the same lines as me by the sounds of it Tom, what if the spirits of the Bartholomew family have been trying to get the attention of all the families that have lived here including the Rodgers family, again a married couple with a child, a daughter. As we now know, it was Wendy that first heard all the banging and dragging sounds coming from the attic. Her parents didn't believe her until Tina Rodgers was tidying up in the bedroom and heard the same thing a few days later...'

'And then both Bill and Tina hear the noises coming from the attic as well as they lay in bed, interjected Tom, they think its Wendy and her friend Jodi messing around up in the attic and Bill gets up to look only to find the attic door locked and then the girls come out of their bedroom, Jodi was having a sleep over, and as they all stand on the landing they hear more loud bangs. At this point Bill Rodgers calls 999 and I arrive with PC Alan Davies, and two other officers and all hell breaks loose.'

'But why the attack on one of your officers by the doll, asked Jack Temple, and the attack on Jane by the doll with the knife?'

'Jane can you remember exactly where you were standing in the kitchen that night?' asked Daniels.

'I'll show you all, come on.' They all followed Jane into the kitchen and she pointed to the side of the fridge which was next to where the Welsh dresser stood before they moved it.

'That's it! By god it's starting to come together now.' cried a triumphant Joseph Daniels. 'Look here, the small indent in the wall, would you say that somehow, whoever was controlling the doll and made the knife move by pure energy alone was trying to show us where the basement was?'

'Come on now Joe, that's madness to think that, the knife was aimed at Jane.' replied a less than enthusiastic Jack

'So why did the knife go into the wall and not Jane, is that the table the knife was on Jane,' Jane nodded in response. 'I think if the spirit of the young girl, which I now firmly believe it is, was trying to kill Jane, she could have done easily, but she didn't, so why not?' replied Daniels.

'Hmm you may have a point there said Father Driscoll, joining in the conversation.

'And furthermore, something else to think about, we have always seen the doll either on the stairs or in the hallway near the stairs, correct, what if we are missing something here, we need to know what is in the basement and then maybe that will give us the answer to why those families fled in fear of their lives and didn't understand!'

'Understand what Joe, spit it out for Christ's sake, sorry about that Father's, said Jack now getting flustered with his team leader.

'In think that somehow in their own way the Bartholomew family are trying to show us something, they have been trying to show every family that has lived here something! Maybe their spirits are trapped and can't rest. Father Gabriel I don't know how much you know about this kind of thing but, if a person is hung for heresy or witchcraft would they be buried in consecrated ground or left to rot where they were hung?' asked Daniels.

'I would say it would be highly unlikely in the days of Oliver Cromwell and Matthew Hopkins that a person hung for heresy would be buried. They would be left to rot and their bodies dumped somewhere, in a well, a river or in a deep hole in a field, why do you ask Joseph.'

'I ask because I think that the family's spirits are wishing for release from the world they are trapped in. They want peace and a proper burial. But sadly we can't do that if we don't know where they were buried can we?'

As the team pondered they all began to hear faint knocking, which began to grow louder and louder. 'Here we go again! It's coming from upstairs, come on.' shouted Joseph. Everyone piled into the spacious hallway and looked up towards the first floor landing, 'What do you want, show us, and we'll help you to be free, that's all we want to do. You have waited long enough for release!' shouted Father Gabriel as both he and Father Driscoll began to ascend the staircase. 'Let us help you as priests, let all of us help you...'

Suddenly there was a loud thunderous crash and all the lights in the house started flicking on and off and the stairs began to vibrate as another loud deafening crash could be heard. The two priests stood rigid as the stairs began to crack open from the top down to the bottom. The large wrought iron chandelier began to sway backwards and forwards, 'Get off the stairs now the chandelier is going to crash down on them at any minute.' Jack Temple shouted as they all feared for the priests' lives. The two priests had seconds to spare, and hit the ground floor running. Moments later the wrought iron light fixture plummeted straight into the middle of the stairs making a massive hole in the middle of them.

The house lay quiet and as the dust around them all settled, they all looked around. 'What was that, some kind of earth tremor?' asked Alexis.

'I think it was the pure energy of three spirits trying to get our attention and it worked, look.' said Superintendent James Fisher As they all looked to where he was pointing they all gasped in unison, at the top of the stairs outside the attic doorway stood three human like shapes that appeared to fade in and out as if their energies were rapidly dwindling. 'Look, whispered Jane, they are all pointing to the middle of the stairs where the chandelier hit,'

Tom looked around and everyone was silent, 'I think they want us to take a look, Alan, come with me mate, let's see what they are pointing at shall we.' As the two policemen slowly made their way up the unsafe stairway, they stopped and looked at the three spirits, 'I think that we are about to help three spirits who are a family and want peace together, come on.' As they got to the centre of the staircase they peered down at the gaping hole the chandelier had made. 'Do you see what I see Tom?' said Alan as he shone his torch into the deep hole under the staircase. 'My god it's another room down there. That's the reason for the entrance way under the stairs; they had two entrances to the basement, not one and two large rooms!'

As they descended the stairs and joined the others they all looked up at the spirits of the Bartholomew family. 'That poor family tried and hung as witches, which they probably weren't. Matthew Hopkins you were the evil one not this family!' shouted Alexis.

The team decided that it would too much of a risk to try and get down the gaping hole and the entrance under the stairs was bricked up solid. They the all heard an almighty bang in the kitchen area and rushed through to see what it was that caused it. Nothing seemed out of place, they then heard it again, this time in the basement. 'I think they are leading us to their burial place.' shouted Joseph as he rushed forward into the basement, no longer afraid, no longer smelling decay, just wanting to help the spirits find peace. 'It's got to be that wall over there.' He shouted as he grabbed a sledgehammer and with all his might he hit the wall dead centre. A multitude of bricks and plaster collapsed instantly to the ground. 'Yes, where through to the other room, now look for any signs of a well in here, search the whole room.'

'A well, why a well Joseph' asked Alexis

'I'll explain all later after we find it, I promise.'

The team searched high and low moving old furniture and other items, they found nothing until something caught Jane's eye, 'What is that over there guys, near the far wall, it looks like a raised stone slab just showing under that large wooden cabinet?'

'By god that could be it, quick everyone let's try and lift it as it looks heavy.' cried out Joseph now starting to feel excited.

Four of the men took a corner of the wooden cabinet each and as one, lifted it and moved it away from the stone slab that lay underneath. 'This could be it Joe, this could be it! Get the crowbars Alan, we're going to need them now!' asked Tom. Alan raced back with them and together both he and Tom pushed the flat ends of the bars under the slab, 'It's moving guys, keep going Alan, that's it we've done it.' Throwing done the crowbars, Tom and Alan pulled out the torches from their pockets and switching them on, shone the beams down into the darkness of the deep well. At the very bottom floated the remains of three bodies. 'I'd say we have found the Bartholomew families remains, wouldn't you Joe?' said Tom as he motioned to Joe to take a look. I'd say you are right with that assumption Tom. Now the family will be able to rest in peace forever. But first of all we need to figure a way to get them out of there as they will need to be buried properly.'

'Leave that job to me everyone; said James Fisher, this is my part in helping the family to rest in peace.' Fisher lifted his mobile phone out of his jacket pocket, 'Hi Superintendent Fisher here, I'm at 215 Lexington Avenue with two of my sergeants and their friends. I need Roger Packard and Julian Edwards here with their block and tackle, and they may need their wet gear too. Yes I want them here straight away, thanks.'

Tom and Alan looked at their boss and in unison said, 'Two of your sergeants' sir?' Fisher just smiled and shook PC Alan Davies by the hand, 'Well I will need a new sergeant once Tom retires won't I and the way you have been throughout this whole thing is amazing, you never once showed fear, I can't think of anyone better suited for the role Alan. Now come on everyone let's get back upstairs and wait for the guys to turn up with the block and tackle. We'll have the family's remains out soon enough.'

As they waited in the living room for Packard and Edwards to turn up, Jack and Jane made two pots of tea and served them out to everyone. Joseph walked out into the hallway and then called the others excitedly to join him. 'Look everyone, look.' He said pointing up to the first floor landing, the dust had now settled and as they looked they could clearly see three solid looking spirit forms looking peacefully down at them.

'My god, I have never ever encountered anything like this in my whole life, this is a very special moment for us all.' said Superintendent James Fisher

'They know they are free now and that they are going to get a proper burial and I think they are showing themselves like that as a thank you for helping them.' said Alexis as she wiped tears from her eyes, 'It's a beautiful sight to behold and one to cherish in our hearts forever.'

Two hours later the remains of all three members of the Bartholomew family were raised from the well, and taken to the coroner's office, where their remains would be cleaned up and then plans for a Christian burial would be performed by Father's Gabriel and Driscoll, both had insisted they would hold the ceremony together and give them a great send off into heaven, where they had always belonged and not dumped in a well.

Chapter Ten

The three policemen, the two priests and the members of the Paranormal Findings group all sat in the comfy living room. Smiles now appearing on their faces after their long ordeal in 215 Lexington Avenue, and now was the time to crack open the bottle of champagne they found in the back of the fridge. 'I'm sure Bill and Tina won't mind once they know the outcome.' said Tom pouring the bubbly liquid into everyone's glasses. 'But how did you know they were trying to show us something Joseph?' asked James Fisher, now warming to the man after guessing right.

'I've been a paranormal investigator for over twenty years James, and in all those years I've helped quite a number of spirits move to the light, be it good spirit or bad. I look for the signs they try to show me while I'm either at home or on an investigation. And the signs in this house were so strong from the very first night we were here, but I couldn't just shout it out, as I didn't know at the time where the basement or the well was. All I kept getting were the words 'basement' and 'well' in my mind's eye. So when Tom told us there was a basement somewhere in the house, I had to trust my instinct and judgement. I don't always get it right, but when I do...'

Everyone raised their glasses in the air and Joseph spoke up loudly, 'A toast to the Bartholomew family may they all rest in peace forever.'

'One thing does puzzle me though Joseph if I may be so bold to ask, said Alexis, why the locked doors on the inside and not on the outside, do you think that happened to the other families that have lived here over the years?'

'Well Alexis if you recall, the first night we were here and Peter got spooked, he ran to the door but it wouldn't open, neither would the back door, Yet when our good friend Alan showed up here with the back-up team, he simply opened the front door and walked in. Now you know most of us tried that door and it wouldn't budge. And when James arrived we were all in the living room when we heard the front door open and found James had just walked in as well, hence the reason for putting the large outdoor flower pots in front of the open door as none of us would have got out...until the end.' They wanted our help desperately and tried everything they could to keep us here. The more frustrated they got the energy they used to control things. They must have known we would be able to help them. Whether it happened to any of the other families only they will know I suppose.'

Epilogue

There were a few more things to tidy up before the team closed the case of 215 Lexington Avenue for good. Tom had promised Bill, Tina and Wendy Rodgers that he would do everything in his power to make things safe again, and the next day after a well-earned rest both he and Alexis drove to Boxley to give them all the good news, but also had to tell them everything that had happened, the remains of the Bartholomew family in the basement well and the destroyed staircase and attic door.

Meanwhile Joseph, Jack and Jane spent a fruitful morning in the town library, they found the full names of the Bartholomew family, and strangely enough their first names were William, Tania and Windy, very close to the Rodgers first names. A full service was held for the family once their names were known and a gravestone was paid for my three certain policemen.

Margaret Rodgers insisted the family stay at her house until their house had been renovated after all that had happened. But Bill had other plans, he just wanted to take his family on holiday away from the nightmare that had been 215 Lexington Avenue, and vowed never to set foot in the house again. The family went on their holiday taking Margaret with them and her 'friend' Monica to keep her company while they were away.

While the Rodgers were enjoying their holiday in Cornwall, Superintendent James Fisher got a call about 215 Lexington Avenue, so did the fire brigade and the ambulance service. Apparently, for some unknown reason, still unknown to this day, the house burnt to the ground. Nothing was left of the house, and since the area was cleared of debris and the well and the basement which being low in the ground was the only room left were filled with tons of cement by a local company. The plot has lain vacant, and probably will for the foreseeable future, but a bench was placed there with a brass plaque on back rest with a dedication to the Bartholomew family, funded by all who helped their spirits move into the light.

Tom Smith retired from the police force and asked Alexis to be his wife, Alexis accepted without hesitation. Everyone that was involved in the case of 215 Lexington Avenue attended the wedding where Alexis announced she was pregnant. Tom started a private paranormal investigative agency with Alexis until she became a mother to their lovely little girl who they named Tania-Windy; he also enlisted the skills of his best buddy Alan Davies, also retired from the police force. When the baby was born James Fisher, nearly retired, was asked to be the baby's godfather an offer he couldn't refuse.

Bill, Tina Rodgers bought a house in Boxley not far from Bill's sister who was now engaged to Monica. Wendy never had any more encounters with the paranormal. Tina gave up teaching and spent more quality time with Wendy and was given a job in Margaret's aromatherapy shop. None of the family bore any scares from the ordeal and neither did any of the team.

Printed in Great Britain
by Amazon